THE BOOKSELLER BLUNDER

A WEAL & WOE BOOKSHOP WITCH MYSTERY

CATE MARTIN

CHAPTER
ONE

August is the one month of the year that doesn't have a major holiday. At least, not in the United States. My birthday wasn't until a week before Halloween, and my uncles weren't due back for another week and a half.

So when I woke up at dawn on a Wednesday in the middle of August, it took me a minute to figure out why I woke up feeling so excited. Like, "it's Christmas morning" excited.

I sat up, put on my glasses, and looked at the time and date on my phone. It was a quarter after six on August 16. But what did that mean?

I was currently in a unique-to-me situation of living somewhere where I actually had close friends. People whose birthdays I would want to celebrate with them. But when I opened up my calendar, I saw that my closest friend Audrey's birthday had happened in May, just before we'd met. Her boyfriend Liam's birthday wasn't until the end of September.

And Steph, in keeping with his usual general air of mystery, had never told me either his age or his birthdate. So it couldn't be him.

I was still frowning at the phone in my hand when the black rat terrier-chihuahua sleeping close to my knees looked up at me through a single open yet still sleepy eye.

Well, the truth was, Houdini only *looked* like a little black dog. So when he used his telepathic power to ask directly into my mind, "What are you looking at, Tabitha?" it was actually a totally unremarkable thing to me.

"I feel like something is special about today, but I don't know what," I said, putting the phone back on my nightstand with a sigh.

Houdini lifted his nose and smelled the air. I involuntarily did the same. The wildfire smoke that had plagued the city all summer was still there, but more of a background flavor now. Mostly what I smelled was the first hints of bread baking in Adrian LeBeau's French Bakery down on the first floor of the Square, the hidden magical neighborhood where I lived in Minneapolis. "The weather is fine. There's that," Houdini said at last.

And it was indeed shaping up to be a perfectly lovely day, sunny and warm without tipping over into either too much heat or too much humidity. Summer in Minneapolis favored tipping into both, in my experience, and this rare bit of pleasant weather was indeed something to be savored.

And yet, that wasn't it.

"It's not *your* birthday, is it?" I asked him.

"Not quite yet," he said, standing up to shake his entire body vigorously. His radar-dish-like ears slapped loudly, and his paws were involuntarily moved away from each other by the ferocity of his shaking. Then he sat back on his haunches with a massive yawn. "Something special about the day. Are you suddenly gaining foretelling powers? Is something *about* to happen?"

"No, nothing like that," I said, tugging at my lip as I wracked my brain.

Then it dawned on me, the sudden flash of inspiration like sunlight pouring into a long-sealed tomb. I blinked a few times, even though this was only a metaphorical burst of light.

I had been so close to figuring it out just before I had thought it might be someone's birthday. Because I truly was in a unique-to-me situation.

"Oh," I said. It sounded so small a word after the impact of the thought that was still echoing through my mind.

"What is it?" Houdini asked, moving closer to put both his front paws on my knee and peer up into my face.

"It's just, this is the longest I've ever been in one place," I told him. "The longest run of nights I've slept in the same bed. The longest time I've known every morning when I wake up that I will see familiar faces all day, and some of them will even be happy to see me."

Houdini mulled this over. Then he said, "It's been two and a half months since we met."

"I know," I said, giving both of his shoulders a vigorous rub. He doesn't like to be petted on the head because he's sensitive about those ears, but he loves a good shoulder rub. He was practically humming with pleasure in the back of my mind.

But he wasn't distracted. "That's not very long in human terms. I mean, my first human Agatha Mirken had lived here in the Square since 1858."

"Believe me, most people are not like Agatha was," I said. Which was an understatement. Even aside from being a very powerful and very long-lived wizard, she had been entirely unique among the other members of the magical community I knew. All of that power and accumulated wisdom, and rather than living in a stone tower devoting her life to the endless pursuit of ever more knowledge—like Steph's master, whom we called only the Wizard—Agatha had run a teashop.

And then she had sacrificed everything to protect Houdini, who wasn't merely a dog who could speak into my mind. Like I said, he only *looked* like a dog. He was, in fact, a baby dragon. That made him a real rarity in our world. One which unscrupulous wizards might try to capture and bend to their will, to take his power for their own.

Since Agatha had gone, protecting him had become my responsibility.

Which was more than a little ironic, since I had even less power than a baby dragon. In truth, far, far less.

But no, I reminded myself as I touched the silver bracelet that hung coolly around my wrist. For years, I had thought I was a witch with no magic. But since coming to live in the Square, I had learned a few things about myself.

I had power enough. Probably too much, if I were being honest.

What I lacked was control. The amulet the Wizard and his apprentice Steph had given me helped, but it wasn't the answer I was looking for.

"Two and a half months is a really short time," Houdini persisted even as I climbed out of the bed and headed to the bathroom.

"It is," I agreed as breezily as I could.

"A *really* short time," he said.

"I already told you all about how many times I changed schools," I said as I turned on the shower. "I mean, I guess I never added them all up, but you must have gotten the picture."

"I never really thought about what it meant in terms of time," he said. "I'm your oldest friend, aren't I? Since Agatha died?"

I would've said it was Agatha's grandniece Audrey who was my oldest friend, because while technically I had known Houdini longer, he hadn't revealed that he could speak to me until after Audrey and I had met. I had truly thought he was the dog he appeared to be, if a particularly high-strung one. But I could sense saying so would hurt his feelings.

So I just agreed, "That's right. You are," as I reached for the moisturizing shampoo that I had bought from the Inanna Salon & Spa the month before. It was made from the finest ingredients from what we witches call the prosaic world—meaning the nonmagical world we exist in the corners of—but the stylist Cressida Cade had juiced those ingredients with a little magic of her own. In my whole life, this was the only thing that kept the literal chaos of my magical powers out of my hair. After rinsing out the conditioner she had also made for me, it was just barely manageable.

Of course, it also helped that the silver amulet Steph and the Wizard had given me had stopped me from randomly sparking power in moments of stress. I hadn't set anything on fire since the beginning of July.

It was no wonder I felt excited about breaking my previous staying-in-one-place record by a single day. I had set my previous record while attending a notoriously dour magical academy that hid deep within the mountains of Antarctica. I was sure (after much careful research on the subject) that H. P. Lovecraft had never actually been there. But after my almost two and a half months there as a student, I would be the first to say he captured the madness of that desolate place really, really well.

But as I toweled my hair dry, I realized it wasn't just the being in one place thing or the sleeping in the same bed thing. It wasn't even just the finally having friends thing, although that was nice.

It was the feeling of being part of a community. As I combed through the hair that wasn't fighting my every stroke, I deeply appreciated what working with a stylist who was familiar with my hair's unique problems could do for me.

And when I went out during my lunch break to pick up some groceries for the week, I knew the Abergavennies would have my favorite brand of Greek yogurt in stock, even though I was the only person in the Square who liked that particular brand (most people think it's too tart, but I like tart).

And if I decided not to cook dinner after closing my uncles' bookshop for the night, I could cross the Square to our local pub where, if the entire crowd didn't shout out my name in greeting, I still got a ton of nods and mug-raises of hello as I came in the door.

"Was it always because of your chaos magic?" Houdini asked with concern as I finished dressing for the day.

"I'm afraid it was," I said. Then I shook the silver bracelet on my wrist at him. "It's nice not to worry about that anymore, I can tell you."

"But you *do* worry," he said. "I can tell you do."

"Well, I worry that I still don't know what my power is and where it came from, or how to use it effectively," I said. Which was the short version of my worry list. But I refused not to feel upbeat on this day that felt like a holiday, if only to me. "But I don't have to worry that I'm a danger to everyone around me because of something I have no hope of being able to control. That's a good thing."

Houdini said nothing as I sat on the edge of the bed to pull on my Converse sneakers.

"Is something bothering you?" I asked when I had both my shoes on and my phone in my pocket. But he was still just watching me with something ineffable in his intelligent brown eyes.

"You must've lived in one place longer than this when you were younger than school age?" he said.

"Maybe," I said. "But you know I don't really remember anything from that time."

That lack of memories of my pre-kindergarten days had gone from something I didn't realize was even a thing to something I vaguely wondered about when I finally realized that most people's memories actually start before the age of five. Finally, meeting my uncle Carlo when I first came to the Square to take the summer job in his bookshop had actually sparked a few dream-like recollections. I knew I had known him at some point in that dark stretch of no memories.

But it wasn't until after everything that had happened on the Fourth of July, when my mother had made her last attempt to sneak into my room in the dead of night to see me in one of those regular encounters I always remembered later as dreams, that I had gotten truly suspicious.

She had done things to make me forget. And the silver bracelet I wore day and night since Steph had given it to me had fended that magic off. She could no longer see me and then make me not remember the details of her visit. For the first week or so after, I had thought only of how that had meant she would likely not come to see me again. Because that thought had been traumatic enough.

It was only long after that night that I started to think that the forgetting she had tried to cast on me was likely related to my lack of early childhood memories.

And I didn't like those thoughts at all. The implications, the hows and whys of it all, they would drive me mad.

And I had no way of knowing what was true.

I still had a few more weeks before my uncles would be home again. They were currently in a rural area in the north of Greece, and prosaic communication was spotty at best. And with so many time zones between Minneapolis and where they were, one of us was always half-asleep when we did speak. No, all my questions about my past and my mother had to wait until he was back again. And even then, I wasn't sure how many of them he would be able to answer.

Because I was pretty sure my mother had put a spell on him too, one that kept him from talking to me about the very things I most needed to know.

And if there was one thing scarier than the thought that my own mother had erased my memories of my early childhood, it was that she had magically gagged my uncle, an adult witch of no small power himself.

I pushed all of those thoughts aside and focused instead on that holiday feeling I had woken up with. It was a small victory, to be sure, but a victory all the same.

And I really wanted to celebrate it with all my friends.

"Come on," I said to Houdini. "Let's go down to the teashop for breakfast. The others will be waiting."

I headed down the first of the many flights of stairs that would take me from the attic room on top of the apartment that sat on top of the seven levels of my uncles' bookshop all the way down to the ground level of the Square, where the Loose Leaves Teashop sat tucked in one corner between the magical and prosaic worlds.

"Do you think Audrey will have more of those biscuit things she baked for me yesterday?" Houdini asked as he zipped along just at my heels. He was a little fellow, but he had the leggy proportions of a horse. The kind that compete in dressage, given his refined pony-like gait.

"I expect she will," I said. "She may be deathly allergic to you, but that doesn't mean she doesn't love you to pieces, you know."

He didn't say anything in my mind, and there was no way to tell by looking at his sweet doggy face, but even so I could sense he was beaming in happy pride as we went out onto my uncles' veranda and started down the cast-iron staircase that would eventually bring us to the teashop.

CHAPTER

TWO

The Loose Leaves Teashop didn't open for business until eight, but Audrey and I had a standing date for breakfast together at seven. Really, this was a carryover from a similar arrangement I had had with her grandaunt Agatha when she had been running the teashop.

The difference was, it wasn't just the two of us. Not anymore. Agatha and I had occasionally had the upstairs neighbor Barnardo Daley come in to pick up an herbal mixture she made for him for reasons neither had ever shared with me, but that was it. Now he was a constant presence at our morning teatime.

As was Audrey's new boyfriend, Liam Kelly.

But the other difference from my time with Agatha was that I really had to make myself scarce at eight. Because, while Agatha had been opening up a shop that few customers ever entered, and was eager for company for as long as I could provide it, that was no longer the case under Audrey's management.

To be fair, Agatha had truly broken her magic when she'd rescued Houdini and hid him in the guise of a dog. Not only were even the most basic of spells beyond her, she had lost the simple ability to brew prosaic tea. That had been really bad for business. So much so that when she died, nearly everyone assumed that Audrey would shut the whole place down, sell the location, and go back to her home in Mankato.

But nothing was calling Audrey back to Mankato. And while her degree in ritual magic had few uses outside of the most selective of covens, which really wasn't Audrey's kind of thing, running a teashop didn't call for much magic at all.

Which is not to say she didn't use any. She had a brisk side business preparing magical teas and tinctures for the residents of the Square. Because while Agatha's many recipes and spells were almost indecipherable to modern eyes, reading and research were two things I was actually good at. I could decipher Agatha's scratchy script and convert the archaic, mostly forgotten language into something Audrey could actually use.

And, boy, could she use it. Her confidence in her own ritual casting ability had grown immeasurably since the day we first met.

The two of us together were an impressive magical team.

But quite apart from that, she had a real talent for running a prosaic business. In just two and a half months, she had turned a shop that most passersby on the Minneapolis street side thought was closed into quite the local attraction. She mixed her own blends of tea and gave them all whimsical names, and the bakery case was always full of treats she baked herself. And now she was adding in special treats just for dogs as well as water bowls she always kept full with cool, clear water, luring in even more of those passersby.

I knew a lot of magic was involved with all of that, although I never came down early enough in the morning to see it happen. Audrey ran the whole teashop herself, including baking all the treats in her display case. In my mind, I pictured Audrey like the Sorcerer's Apprentice directing all the kitchen implements to work together to the waving beat of her wand, but without the disastrous turn of events from the movie because she never lost control.

But again, not that I ever saw it. Dawn was quite early enough for me to be waking up, thank you very much. I didn't know how Audrey could do it, getting up at four in the morning every day. But I knew she did it well.

And with a smile, always. As Houdini and I came in the door that morning, she was already directing that smile my way from where she stood behind the counter, sliding a tray of scones onto the top shelf of her display case.

"What's the special today?" I asked, looking through the sparkling glass at all the freshly baked goodness below it.

"For sweet, it's sticky orange scones, and for savory, it's white cheddar and chive scones," she said. Then she tucked the swinging sides of her long, straight blonde hair behind her ears, a gesture so familiar it made something in my chest swell a little in fondness.

I was having all the feels today, that was for sure. But it wasn't a bad thing, appreciating all over again how nice it was to have someone smile when I came in the room, genuinely happy to see me.

"Any biscuits for me?" Houdini asked almost shyly as he looked up at her from the floor by my ankle.

"A new recipe," Audrey told him. "Pumpkin and peanut butter. I think you're going to like it."

"I know it's for dogs, but it sounds good to me too," Liam said as he emerged from the back room with a heavily laden tea tray. I opened the door in the counter for him and he gave me a nod of thanks before carrying the tray through to our customary table by the window on the Square side of the shop. As he started distributing the cups and saucers, Audrey handed me a serving platter of scones, the sticky orange on one side and the white cheddar and chives on the other.

"You spoil us," I said to her, and she blushed furiously.

"Actually, Liam made the tea today," she rushed to say.

"Really?" I said, turning to see his peaches-and-cream complexion blushing nearly as deeply as hers. His hair might be curlier and a darker blonde, and his eyes were a lighter shade of blue, but basically the two of them were like a matched set. And since they made their dating official, their bouts of blushing had been off the charts.

"It's just a blend of orange pekoe with ginger, nutmeg and a little brown sugar syrup," he said. "I thought it would go nicely with the sticky orange scones." He set the massive teapot on the center of the table with a flourish. It was just a silver teapot, minimalist in design, if large in size.

I had liked the tea service that Audrey and I had always used when it was just the two of us, a blue and white China pattern that had depicted scenes out of something like *The War of the Worlds*. They had certainly been Agatha's favorite. But there had only been two cups in that set, and the teapot hadn't held any more than two cups' worth of tea.

There were more of us meeting for breakfast these days. Liam was there every morning now, without fail.

And so was Barnardo Daley, I thought even as he came in through the door that opened out onto the Square, his black-haired Siamese Miss Snooty Cat in his arms. Houdini looked up at the cat with a pronounced bristling of the hair along his spine, but his mouth was too full of Audrey's pumpkin and peanut butter treats to muster up a growl at her.

A fact which all of us silently shared thanks for as we sat down at the table.

"Good morning, all," Barnardo said to us as he slid into his usual spot and spread a cloth napkin over his lap. His tan pants and white button-up shirt were already covered in a multitude of black cat hairs, but I suppose he didn't want to add dribbles of tea or scone crumbs to what could otherwise be taken care of with a good lint brush.

Barnardo lived in the apartment directly over the teashop. He was older than the rest of us at the table by about a decade, and he tended to dress like a prosaic who worked in a high-end accounting office, albeit an accountant who was always covered in cat hair.

What his actual job was, I still didn't know. He had a way of dodging that question whenever I tried to bring it up.

I wasn't even sure what magic he could do, besides a few small spells that all seemed related to entertaining. When he was in charge of a party, no food in a buffet would ever taste like it sat under the warming lights too long, and the ice in his cooling buckets never melted.

Reserved as he was about his private life, he was a pleasant companion. It was just a shame that the only other person in his life was, in fact, his cat.

And Miss Snooty Cat earned every bit of that name. Houdini might be quick to object to others for very little reason—the barking thing we had just narrowly avoided a moment ago was all too common with him—but in the case of Barnardo's cat, I was a hundred percent behind Houdini. If it was socially acceptable for me to bark at her every time I met her, I would be tempted to do it, too.

Audrey finally emerged from behind the counter with a bowl of fruit salad, and Liam and I sat down the same moment she did. Scones were passed around and Liam poured out the tea. I managed to hold up my end of the various murmured "thanks" and "here you go"s, but my eyes kept going back to the cup and saucer next to mine. The ones waiting in front of the still-empty chair.

Audrey and Liam always set a place out for Steph, even though most days he never showed. It looked like this was going to be one of the most days.

It was so very usual a bit of business, I really had no place feeling disappointed. And yet I did. I still felt like it was a personal holiday for me, as much as I didn't want to bring up the how and why with the others. I just wished he was there.

Well, I wished that a lot.

"These scones are perfection, Audrey," Barnardo said. Audrey blushed her way through more thanks, because we all knew he meant what he said. Barnardo took culinary delights too seriously to ever force out a compliment he didn't mean.

"They are quite good, aren't they?" I said. "And they pair so well with the tea."

"I know orange pekoe isn't really orange flavored," Liam felt compelled to clarify. "Actually, I have no idea why they call it that. Isn't it a black tea?"

"It is," Audrey told him. "Orange pekoe is the name for the grade of tea leaf. Which isn't orange flavored or orange colored. It might be related to the House of Orange, but as with so many historical things, the real story is probably lost to time."

"A mystery a little out of our purview," Barnardo said with a wistful sigh.

"You won't catch me lamenting a lack of murders lately," I said.

"No, of course not," he said, too quickly.

But I wasn't being entirely truthful, either. Not that I wished for people to die. Quite the opposite.

But having a mystery to investigate really broke up the long days minding the bookshop.

As I had cause to remember again after Houdini and I had made ourselves scarce so Audrey could open the teashop and start her day. Liam had not one but two interviews for possible jobs that day, and even Barnardo had seemed anxious to get back to whatever it was that filled his days.

I turned the sign on the bookshop door from *closed* to *open*. I checked the most recent page of the magic tome that linked our magical bookshop with similar shops all around the world, a network that assisted us all in matching buyers and sellers of rare tomes, and found no new requests since the last one nine days before. Then I logged into our web store and checked for online orders.

There weren't any.

After that, there was little to do but wait for customers to turn up.

And on a Wednesday, there were usually few enough of those.

I was a jumble of emotions. I was still feeling strangely up with that personal holiday vibe. But I was also sort of wistfully sad that Steph had missed breakfast.

I looked at the stack of books I had pulled from the shelves the day before, intending to browse through them today, but a quick scan of the titles on the spines wasn't filling me with confidence that they would have any more secrets about chaos magic lurking in their pages than any of the similar stacks I had gone through over the past month. That was triggering something between disappointment and anxiety, a weird muddy feeling like they were paint colors I should never have tried mixing together.

Shoehorning a general sense of boredom into that emotional morass was going to be a weird fit. And yet there it was, jamming its way into my mind.

Then I noticed that, as weirdly emotional as I was, something was also going on with Houdini. Only his feelings seemed to be all down. Even his tail and his ears were drooping.

"Houdini? What's wrong?" I asked.

"Nothing," he said glumly.

"I don't believe that. Did you eat too many of Audrey's dog treats?"

Not that I would blame him. They had smelled really good. And my own tummy was a bit uncomfortably full. I regretted that third sticky orange scone.

That's a lie. I regretted nothing. It had been both sticky and orange as well as baked perfection.

But I fought back the wave of food nostalgia for breakfast and stayed focused on Houdini.

"It really is nothing," he said. "I think I'll just pop up to the nook and take a little nap."

"Are you sure?" I asked. "I mean, you do have a bed down here, too."

"Yes, thank you, I do appreciate that," he said with stiff formality. "But today I think I will nap in the nook. If that's all right with you?"

"Of course," I said, but something stabbed at my heart as I

watched him make his way slowly up the stairs, his normally corkscrewed tail hanging limply behind him.

Houdini never did anything slowly. And his philosophy was "Why just run all over the place if you can parkour?" It was like I was watching a whole different dog. Or, rather, a whole different baby dragon in the guise of a dog.

But as I settled onto the tall stool behind the former apothecary counter that was the bookshop's front desk, I decided he wasn't going upstairs to avoid me.

Not that I had ever seen it happen, but I had had cause in the past to suspect that the nook on the fourth floor—my special place to read, study, and research, the one that always magically provided whatever I needed just before I realized I needed it—also performed a similar function for Houdini.

I knew he could read. The text wasn't the problem for him; it was turning the pages. But for an enchanted space that could conjure a bowl of chalk out of nothingness the minute I wanted to write something on the slate wall that ran along one side of the nook, magically turning pages for a dog to keep reading had to be like nothing.

That only left the question as to what Houdini was researching that he didn't want to share with me. I knew he was longing to find his birth family again, and I had tried helping him find out anything at all. But while the bookshop contained multitudes of books about dragons, they were all general texts about their biology or history or appearances in prosaic mythologies. There was nothing that would tell us anything about living dragons who might be Houdini's kin.

But perhaps he thought I had given up the search too soon.

I looked again at the stack of books, almost doomed to tell me nothing new about chaos magic. A search just as hopeless as his. And just as depressing. If he needed time alone to pursue something he would have to rationally agree was unlikely to bear fruit, who was I to judge?

But even as I pulled the top book off the stack and started turning the pages, I couldn't shake the feeling that his depression had some other trigger. It hadn't been there when we woke up that morning. Was it just coming back inside the bookshop that had him down?

Lunchtime rolled around, and Houdini was still up in the nook. I turned the sign to *closed* just long enough to make my grocery run, then put everything away in the kitchen of my uncles' apartment. A kitchen that still reminded me strongly of a ship's galley. Small space, used to maximum efficiency. I was trying to keep it as neat and organized as my uncle Carlo always kept it, but I was only partly succeeding. I made a quick sandwich, promised myself I would clean up the crumbs before going to bed, and headed back down to open the bookshop again.

As slowly as the morning had passed, the afternoon passed even more slowly. I could hear a clock ticking, which was maddening, since I had no idea where inside that bookshop we even had a clock. Was I just imagining it? I was tempted to leave the desk to find it, but knowing how the bookshop could grow entire new alcoves just to amuse itself, I didn't risk it. It felt like bait for a trap, to lure me away from my only responsibility.

As if the bookshop were as bored as I was, and looking for a little amusement at my expense.

Not that it would have mattered if I had left the front desk. When six o'clock finally rolled around and I went to lock the door and turn the sign one last time, it was at the end of a long, slow day without a single customer to break up the monotony.

My uncles dealt in magical books more than prosaic ones. And magical book sales tended to be few and far between, but incredibly lucrative when they happened. The prosaic side of the business was really just because my uncle Carlo was fond of prosaic culture.

The fact that his husband Frank was a prosaic himself was probably related to that.

I felt another stab of lonesomeness at the few memories I had formed of the two of them before they had gone on their long-delayed honeymoon and book- and artifact-buying trip. But they would be back soon enough. And then even customer-free days would still involve at least their company.

I had just adjusted the sign so that it hung a little straighter in the window when I felt something behind me. Something so subtle I wasn't even sure which of my senses had detected it. I hadn't heard or seen anything, and the only smell in the air was the usual bouquet of bookshop aromas I loved so much.

And yet, I knew something had just displaced the air behind me.

Which meant only one thing.

I spun around, a grin already on my face, all lonely and sad thoughts gone from my mind as if they had never been.

There, standing between me and the desk, was Stephanos Underwood. He was, as always, dressed all in black like a modern day Hamlet, save for the long, multicolored robe with its eye-catching iridescent sheen. That robe was moving around him as if it felt a wind that I did not. Even the tangle of dark curls of hair on top of his head was in motion.

But this always happened when he teleported into the bookshop. I had no idea what the experience of teleporting without walking through a portal felt like, never having done it myself. But it seemed to involve more wind machines than a Bollywood movie.

"Steph," I said, and tried really hard to dial my smiling face down a few degrees. But I was pretty sure I failed.

"Oh good, you're closed," he said. He sounded kind of breathless, like he'd run here, stairs and all.

"It's six o'clock," I said. "I was just about to grab some dinner."

"Dinner," he repeated, as if the word had a sudden new meaning for him. "I haven't eaten all day."

"I have the makings of tuna casserole upstairs. I could have it ready in an hour. Unless you want to hit the pub?" I said, alternating pointing my thumbs up towards the attic apartment or directly in front of me towards the back of the bookshop, beyond which lay the pub.

As if he didn't know where these places were.

"That sounds great, but there's something I need to do first. And I think you need to come with me," he said with a gleam to his eye that I would swear was mischievous, if I thought for a minute he ever gave in to such impulses.

"Where?" I asked.

"A village high in the Pyrenees Mountains," he said casually.

"The Pyrenees Mountains?" I asked. I honestly wasn't sure if he was joking. I mean, he had to be joking. The gleam in his eye was definitely up to *something*.

But as long as I'd known him, Steph had never been joking about anything.

"I need to pick up a book. A *magic* book," he added, raising his eyebrows for emphasis.

"I mean," I said, lifting my hands to encompass the bookshop full of magic books that we were, in fact, standing in at that very moment.

But he just stepped closer to me, close enough to whisper directly into my ear. Which made it hard to focus on his words, as I was again distracted by the fact that I always tasted butterscotch when he was near.

Not smelled, tasted.

How did he do that?

But then the words he was breathing warmly into my ear became impossible not to hear.

"A very particular magic book," he said. "I'm talking about a rare —dare I say *banned*?—tome of chaos magic."

Then he pulled back to grin at me, and the mischief that had lurked in his eyes was all over his face now.

And just like that, my day became the very opposite of boring.

CHAPTER

THREE

N ow, since coming to the Square, I had seen Steph appear and disappear several times. Being able to teleport without using the inherent strong magics of an established portal is a rare skill. I was pretty sure that he, young as he was, only managed it because of magic woven into that multicolored robe.

And I had assumed that the robe belonged to the Wizard, because every time I had seen Steph teleport in or out of a place, it had always been while doing some of the Wizard's business.

But this favor for me, was it also something the Wizard considered his business?

According to Steph, the Wizard was very interested in helping me master my chaos magic. But I have to say "according to Steph" because I had yet to actually meet the Wizard myself. Or even perceive a doorway into his home, the Tower.

So when Steph held out a hand for me to take, I suddenly found myself incapable of just slipping my hand into his.

"Is this going to get you into trouble?" I asked.

"Not remotely," he said.

"So the Wizard is sending you on this mission?" I asked.

That grin was back. But shrugging, he said, "He's deep in his meditation practices for a problem he's focused on. Not only would he not mind me using his robe to take you to a remote mountain village on the far side of the planet for a very short trip, he would very much object to me interrupting him to ask for permission."

"Maybe we should wait until we *can* ask," I said.

"Normally, that's what I would do," he said. And suddenly the grin fell away from his face. I felt a little bad that I was killing the joy of his small act of rebellion. But the very last thing I wanted was to end up on the wrong side of the Wizard.

"So—" I started to say, but stopped when I realized Steph was still talking.

"What we're going to look for is likely going to be there for a very limited time," he said. "Look, I can't bring us directly into the village. There are rules about this sort of travel. I have to bring us to an abandoned pasture a little north of the village, and then we have to walk in. I can explain everything on the way from the pasture to the bookshop, I promise. But we do have to hurry. I don't think the guy we're going to meet is the kind who's willing to wait."

Then he beckoned me again with his still outstretched hand.

I took his hand, and that butterscotch taste on my tongue intensified, like the buttery sweetness of a real candy was melting over my tastebuds. The minute my hand was in his, he tucked me close at his side, whisking the floating folds of his multicolored robe around us both. A spicy smell washed over me as well as a delicious warmth. It was like there was an entirely different atmosphere inside that garment.

"Ready?" he asked, his dark brown eyes gazing down at me.

"Ready," I said. Which was a total lie. I had never teleported anywhere in my life by myself, only as someone's passenger through a portal. I had no idea what this experience was even going to be like, let alone if I was in any meaningful way "ready" for it.

Then his arms tightened around me, and the folds of the robe closed in over my head. I was in darkness, but it was a warm, comfortable darkness. I could feel Steph breathing, even sense his heartbeat. I could hear a sound like sails slapping in a wind.

Then the feeling of having ground beneath my feet just... went away.

I let out an involuntary eep of dismay. This didn't feel like flying or falling or even just floating, all things I had done before thanks to various spells cast by other students in my schooldays. It was completely different, completely alien to my experience.

All I knew was that I very much wanted the feel of the ground back.

But as soon as I had formed that thought, my wish was granted. I was just registering the sense that the ground under me was not level like the carpeted floor of the bookshop entryway, when Steph flipped back the edges of the robe. I flinched out of reflex, expecting the sudden blinding light of the sun after a long day stuck mostly indoors.

But we had traveled to the Pyrenees, and in the Pyrenees, it was the middle of the night. Just past one in the morning, to be specific. My uncles had been in Spain for a couple of weeks, and I was familiar with the time difference from the nights when I had tried to call them.

I looked around, drinking in the view. Stars shone brightly in the cloudless sky overhead, more stars than I had seen in the night sky since I had left my last magical academy to go to Minneapolis. That had been in the Carpathian Mountains. But this was my first time in Spain, if we were in fact in Spain. If we were in France, I had never been to this part of it. Only Paris and, very briefly but memorably, in Dieppe.

Nothing around me gave me any clue as to where we were precisely. Just alpine meadows of waving grass with rocky peaks above, now mere silhouettes blocking the stars beyond.

But looking downhill, I could see the lights of a village a short walk from where we stood.

"It's one in the morning here," I said. "That's when this guy agreed to meet us?"

"Oh," Steph said. Then he chuckled to himself. "Sorry, I didn't think through our dinner plans. I doubt any place I was thinking of will be open at this hour."

"And the meeting?" I asked, trying not to let the sudden stab of disappointment that was piercing my chest reflect in my voice.

"That's not a problem," Steph said. "We *do* have an appointment, I swear. I've been in contact with the man all day. He came across the tome this morning and knew the Wizard had been putting the word out for such things. He wants to unload it as soon as possible. Illegal, remember? So it's not exactly strange that he would only meet after hours. And he *was* the one who set the time. But we should get going. I'm not sure if he's going to have any patience for us being late. We've been communicating by magic parchment, so all I have to go on is his written word, but he seemed very nervous. Almost edgy. I don't think he'll wait if we're late."

"Of course, let's hurry, then," I said.

Steph looked around briefly, then indicated a direction with a jut of his chin. I followed along beside him, only realizing that he had seen a stony footpath through the tall, dry grasses when we stumbled onto it.

"What country are we in?" I asked as we walked. The air was chilly for August, but considering our current altitude, that was hardly surprising. Still, I wished I had gone up to my bedroom for a jacket before embarking on this journey.

"You know, I'm not actually sure," he said. "This village has existed for centuries, and life here has gone on largely untouched by the rest of the world for most of that. But technically, politically, it belonged to a variety of kingdoms, empires, and countries over that time. I'm not sure it matters to the people who live here. To them, it is merely Herri."

"Doesn't that just mean 'village'?" I asked. "Or I guess any kind of a geographic collection of people. Nation, country, town, whatever."

He only gave me a brief sideways glance, and it was a dark, moonless night. But I didn't miss the look in his eyes. He was impressed.

And I felt warmer in a way that had nothing to do with the walking.

"I believe it does," he said. "I've only been here twice before, on totally unrelated missions for the Wizard."

"So, this is a magical community?" I asked. It was barely a question, I was so sure the answer was yes. Existing for centuries without change, unconcerned with prosaic politics? It was a statement uplifted at the end only as a conversational "back to you" cue.

And yet, to my surprise, Steph was shaking his head. "Yes and no," he said at last. "The population is almost equal parts of each. And they coexist almost openly, with no real conflict."

"*Almost* openly?" I said.

"Tourists are rare, but they do pass through. The state of things here is not open to their experience," he said. "You should see the marketplace during the day. Farmers sell their produce side by side with witches selling potions and amulets, and no one bats an eye."

"I would like that," I said. "I wonder if my uncles passed through here? They took a circuitous path from Spain to Greece, but beyond some tucked away mountain towns in the north of Italy they told me about, I'm not sure just where they were."

"It would be a good bet they came through here, given the nature of the shopping they were looking to do," Steph said.

"So they've been to the bookshop here?" I asked.

The path suddenly became so steep that the rocky top layer went from an annoyance to walk on to an actual treacherous challenge. As careful as I was, I could feel the pebbles under the soles of my sneakers sliding away, threatening to dump me on my butt. I managed to stay on my feet, but barely.

Then we were on a well-maintained cobblestone road. The stones glowed in the starry night like they were coated with silver, and the road itself seemed wider than it needed to be. But perhaps that was just because, being the middle of the night, we were the only ones on it. With other pedestrians, perhaps a couple of rows of carts going to and fro, it would likely be a different story.

What was odd was, as much as it looked like the only road that ran through the entire length of the narrow town, there wasn't a single sign of a motorized vehicle. Not so much as a scooter or motorcycle, let alone a car. Granted, I could see the far side of the village from where we were standing. This was the very definition of a walkable town.

But still. They had to get down off the mountain sometime. So where did they park?

With all those thoughts running through my head, it took me a long time to realize that Steph hadn't answered my question. But unlike me, it wasn't because he had gotten distracted by the sight of the village, which looked like something out of a fairy tale book. The white walls of the buildings glowed softly in the starlight. The exposed timbers of their frames and their many open shutters looked colorless in the darkness, but as we drew closer to one and then another, I suspected a shade of red I would love to see by daylight. And being a mountain town, the slanted roofs were all built to withstand heavy snowfalls.

But I adjusted my view as we walked. It was fairytale-like, surely. But more than that, it looked like something built in a theme park to bring a fairy tale to life. It even seemed to be scaled ever so slightly down from normal people height, all the doorways just a little lower and a little narrower than I was used to.

But there I was, getting all distracted again. I live in a world of magic, true enough, but the prosaic world has its own wonders, and I'm prone to raptures of delight. I admit it.

Meanwhile, Steph was practically radiating mental discomfort. Enough where I finally did notice it.

"What is it?" I asked him.

"I should probably tell you before we get there," he said. "This isn't the sort of bookshop your uncles would ever go to procure things."

"I'm not even sure what that would mean," I said. I couldn't imagine what sort of bookshop my uncles wouldn't go into. They were as at home in a prosaic bookshop as a magical one, and didn't even seem bothered to find themselves in the sort of niche bookshops that catered to very specific interests.

I mean, they had gone all the way to the UK just to visit a bookshop that only sold books about trains. Unlike the UK, Minnesota barely even *has* trains beyond the cargo-hauling variety. But still.

"I feel like at this point I should say yet again that the Wizard, while not knowing specifically where I'm taking you, wouldn't have had a problem with it if he did," Steph said.

"Wow, are you waffling so hard," I said. "Stop spinning it and tell me where we're going, please."

"It's going to look like a prosaic bookstore that focuses on.... adult subject matter," he said with great reluctance.

I just avoided laughing out loud, which would've shattered the quiet of the night around us. But it was a close thing.

"Is that all?" I said. "I mean, ew. But you had me really worried we were going somewhere, I don't know, *illegal*."

"Well, that's the thing," he said. "The prosaic bookstore is a front. What we're looking for is going to be in the back. Behind the counter. So to speak."

"Oh," I said. "So you brought me to an illegal backdoor business at one in the morning, and if we get picked up by local law enforcement, we don't even know what country they represent?"

"More or less," he said. "But it's going to be fine, I promise you."

"Because you have an appointment?" I asked.

"Because we have an appointment," he agreed.

"And you've worked with this person before. On behalf of the Wizard," I said. Again, not really a question in my head.

But it should've been. Even in the dark, I could see the pale skin of his cheeks flush.

"Not this person, no," he admitted. "But I was put in touch with this person by the Wizard's local contact. And it's her business we're using for the meeting. She's a mutual acquaintance of the seller and the Wizard both. Well, I know her a little too."

"So that's okay, then," I said. I was trying for a cheery tone, but those words came out too aggressively for that.

"I've explained before that chaos magic is forbidden," he said, speaking close to my ear in another one of his warm whispers. As if even here, in this sleeping mountain village, it would be dangerous for us to be overheard. "You must've guessed that finding books on the topic, ones that survived all the censors and book burnings over the centuries, would involve going to some shady places."

"You're right," I was forced to agree. "I didn't really think it through, but of course you're right. But you're sure we're safe?"

"As long as you're with me, you're safe," he said, even raising his hand to make a little salute, as if those words were an oath.

Somehow, those words *did* make me feel better.

Then Steph guided me off the wide starlit street, down a darkened alley to a backdoor that was even shorter and narrower than the ones that opened up onto the main street, and *safe* was pretty far down the list of things I was feeling. Closer to the top were things like cold, nervous, lightheaded from the altitude, hungry.

Like we were being watched. Although when I peered into the shadows around us, I saw nothing peering back. But still.

But mostly, what I felt could be summoned up in a single thought.

This had better be worth it.

FOUR

Steph signaled for me to stay back in the shadows of the narrow alley, a command I had no problem complying with. Being able to see the silvery shine of the cobblestones of the main road down the end of the long, dark tunnel of the alley was a real plus in my book. Even so, he gave me an apologetic smile for how the evening was progressing before turning away from me to step up on the uneven stoop of the shop's back door.

Then he drew himself up to his full height, moved his hands through his hair in a way that had to be intended to muss up more than smooth down, given the end state, and only then knocked briskly on the door.

The wood of that door must be quite thick, the sound was so muffled to my ears. Steph stepped back off the stoop just as that door started to swing out towards him, then waited politely just out of the path of the door.

A door which was, indeed, almost crazily thick. Like someone had molded the wood of a normal-sized door like clay, sculpting it down to fit the doorway that was both shorter and narrower than the door was made for, leaving it thicker in the end.

I mean, crazily thick unless there was a reason to expect this door would need to withstand battering rams on a regular basis. Which it totally could. I suspected it would be easier to break through the wall.

"You're late," said a gravelly voice that I only belatedly realized was coming from a woman. She stepped out far enough to stand in the doorway, but with the light behind her, I could only make out her silhouette.

But that was enough to see this was definitely a woman, one tall enough to need to bend down to poke her head through the doorway, and one wide enough to need to turn sideways if she intended to actually pass through it into the scrubby little yard where Steph was standing in the scattering of light that made it out from around her body.

I mean, the round arms that caught the light behind her weren't overtly feminine, but the mass of bosom between them definitely was.

"I think you'll find I'm right on time, Miss Hippolyta," Steph said, with a little sketch of a bow. "And I've brought the buyer with me. Is the seller here?"

"He's waiting," said the woman. "Hippolyta" I believed. She totally looked like a Hippolyta. But "Miss?" Her gravelly, almost sullen voice sounded like it came from the kind of woman that would destroy a grocery store bag boy for calling her "miss."

She poked her head out further through the doorway, but in doing so, her wide shoulders blocked even more of the light coming from behind her. Her face was as much of a mystery to me as ever.

But I thought I could make out her eyes. They were the gleaming things fixed steadily on mine.

"Why is your seller lurking in the shadows, young master?" she asked. I was pretty sure those eyes were still on mine, but narrowed now in suspicion.

I just managed to swallow down what would've been my second eep of the evening.

"Because you haven't invited us in yet," Steph said, blithely unbothered.

Miss Hippolyta grunted at that, as if thoroughly unimpressed. But she stepped back, finally letting the light behind her fall across the stoop like a golden welcome mat.

"Shall we?" Steph said, extending his hand to me again. I took it far more readily than I had the first time, and was only a tiny bit disappointed that he merely tucked it around his arm at the elbow and didn't pull me in close beside him again like before.

I mean, I could really use the warm comfort of that robe around me now. And not just because the thin mountain air had gotten so cold while I was standing still that I was actively shivering now.

We slipped through the narrow doorway into an even tinier space that was mostly cluttered with a heavy coat on a hook, an assortment of hats and scarves on other hooks, and two different pairs of boots, one pair clearly for rain and the other, thicker, fur-lined pair for snow. They were all sized to fit the woman who had already slipped out of sight, once more blocking the light from the room beyond and leaving no impression save for her massive silhouette.

"She's human, right?" I whispered to Steph, a lame attempt at a joke.

"Mostly," he said, which was not comforting at all.

But then he squeezed my hand on his arm, and *that* totally was.

Steph led us out of the coatroom toward the light that turned out to be coming from a single bare lightbulb hanging low from a beam that ran across the slanted ceiling overhead. The entire space was a sort of lean-to built against the back of the main building; I recognized that the vertical red timbers on my right matched those on the front of the building.

The rest of the walls were thin boards nailed to a minimal supporting structure built from two by fours. Not that any of it looked *new*. No, as much as the building we were in the back of had been around for centuries—easily—this added space was only modern by comparison. I guessed it was still decades older than me.

Miss Hippolyta moved around a large, heavy desk that barely left enough room for her to squeeze through. The hanging bulb was behind her now, almost brushing against the back of her head, and I could see thick waves of golden hair that were only just starting to be touched by gray. That hair fell to her waist, which was encircled with the sort of thick, heavy leather belt that dwarves in movies tended to wear.

That, or power lifters who needed the back support.

Her pants were nondescript, some dark color it was hard to discern, given the reach of the light was being obscured by the heavy desk as well as her own upper body. But I could easily make out the faded, once-white shirt that was just barely avoiding bursting at the seams every time she moved her arm, first to shift the desk chair out of her way, then move a broom that was leaning impractically against the closed door on the other side of the room, and finally to knock briefly on that door.

I shifted my weight from foot to foot and noticed the floor under me had a strange give to it. I looked down at a startlingly new Persian rug, the vivid greens and blues and yellows of its woven pattern lovely even in the unkind light from the bulb.

I was pretty sure there was a trapdoor under that rug. And Steph and I were standing on it.

"Storage," he whispered to me, his breath warm against my ear. "Not a trap."

Then he pulled back enough so that I could see the reassuring smile he was giving me.

"Cellars aren't great for books," I said. Which I hadn't failed to notice there weren't any of in the room we were standing in.

"Books aren't really my bread and butter, as you people say," Miss Hippolyta said in a low growl as she moved the desk chair a second time before settling into it with a satisfied groan. She definitely had an accent, but I couldn't place where it was from. It didn't sound French or Spanish, and despite my little show for Steph earlier, I didn't really know much Basque. But I didn't think that was where her accent was from, either. I guessed she was no more a local than we were.

Which only added to my questions about her. But I dragged my mind back to the relevant things in the present and not her no doubt mysterious past.

"So, what *is* down there?" I asked. A little too eagerly, perhaps, because as she sat back in the chair and I got my first good look at her face, it was to see two thick eyebrows raised high, as if she was pondering whether or not to take offense. "Sorry. Not my business," I rushed to say. Then I bit down on both of my lips, determined not to say another word. It would be better if Steph took the lead, since this was a person he both knew and did business with at least semi-regularly. I didn't want to ruin a needed contact for him or the Wizard.

Not that Steph seemed bothered by any of the conversation. All of his attention was focused on the door barely visible behind the girth of Miss Hippolyta.

For my part, I couldn't take my eyes off her. Partly I was waiting to see how she would react, whether she was going to fall on the side of taking offense or shrugging my words off as a mere faux pas. But mainly I was trying to work out just what she was. Human, mostly, like Steph had said, I was pretty sure of that. But there was something else there as well, something that I could almost guess at, but not quite. There were quite a number of beings who had cross-bred with magical humans, if not frequently. Knowing where she was really from would be a start.

I wished I had my books with me. A little quick cross-referencing would be so illuminating right now.

But I pushed the urge aside and forced my mind to focus.

"Indeed," Miss Hippolyta said at last, apparently deciding to fall on the side of not being offended. Then she leaned forward in her chair just as the door behind her—the one she had knocked on the moment before—opened up. "No, I do believe *this* is your business now."

She turned as much as she could in the chair that hadn't exactly been built to fit her, watching as someone slipped into the room like a thief or a cutthroat, keeping to the shadows.

Not that he had much choice. Not with Miss Hippolyta blocking most of the light. Still, it felt like he was flowing from darkest patch to darkest patch, stopping at a point between the edge of the desk and the timbered walls of the back of the shop. A point that was still somehow in shadow despite the unblocked presence of the bulb.

I was still biting down on both my lips, but now I was also lecturing myself not to jump to any prejudiced conclusions about people. There were all sorts of magic types who find light onerous, and while some enjoy exploiting the prosaic world's superstitions about things like vampires to make themselves feel powerful or mysterious, others are far more benign.

I mean, I was pretty sure that Volumnia, the old witch who took care of the dead back in the Square, never came out during the light of day, preferring the cool darkness of her catacombs. And while she still could give me chills if I looked at her too long with her eerily bright eyes, I had also come to trust and rely on her as a valued member of our community.

This man could be much the same for this community, for all I knew. I should at least give him a chance. Even if he seemed to be going out of his way to make sure I couldn't get a good look at him.

I was thinking all that, right up until Steph slipped my hand off his arm, then moved me by my shoulders until I was standing on the far side of him. He tucked my hand back over his arm, and the calm, almost bored look on his face was telling everyone in the room that nothing of import had just happened.

But I could feel the new tension of his arm under my hand. I knew he had just put himself between me and something he sensed was a potential danger.

And I knew that somewhere under that robe was his ebony

wand, and his arm remained tense because he held his hand at the ready to draw it out in a flash if needed.

But he just smiled benignly at Miss Hippolyta and the shadows where the newcomer lurked both.

"I notice you didn't bring it with you," Steph said.

"Couldn't very well, could I?" the man in the shadows said. I sensed danger there in his voice, but not the danger of evil intent. More the danger of a cornered animal who's prepared to strike to get away. "I told you, I don't know where it came from or how it got in my parents' shop. I just want to be rid of it. I certainly don't want to be caught carrying it around."

Then he stepped forward, just half a step, not enough to be properly in the light. But I could make out his eyes, wider than normal, with the whites visible almost all the way around. And the pupils were jumping around as he constantly moved from looking at Steph to me to Miss Hippolyta then back again.

"We didn't discuss taking two meetings. In fact, given the circumstances, that feels very risky indeed," Steph said gravely. Miss Hippolyta made a grunting sound that might have been in agreement, or might have just been her dinner repeating on her.

"Risky to you, perhaps. Not to me," the man said. I could just detect motion in that shadow, as if he were wringing his hands.

"Taking the book away was going to reduce the risk to you, wasn't it?" Steph said reasonably. "That was the entire purpose."

"You weren't doing this as a favor to *me*," the man all but spat. "You were doing it for *her*."

And with that he lunged forward out of the shadow, his trembling hands gripping the scarred wood of the desktop so tightly the knuckles of his already pale fingers went completely bloodless. But there was definitely blood in his eyes. The whites I had seen in the shadows were rimmed with red, and shot through with a spiderweb of burst blood vessels. His hair had missed so many washings it wasn't possible to tell what color it truly was, particularly not in the light from the bulb overhead, but it burst out from his scalp in crazy clumps like the hair of a cartoon mad scientist.

But most alarming of all was his clothing. Like his hair, it had clearly gone far too long without cleaning or attention of any kind. But something recent had definitely happened to it. Bits of it were singed, the charred edges so freshly damaged they crumbled into ash even as he moved.

And the smell of smoke was thick in the air. I knew it was coming from his clothes, but what I smelled wasn't burned cotton or wool or other fabric.

He smelled of burned *books*.

And it broke my heart.

Steph didn't look at me, but he sensed my distress all the same. He casually put an arm around my shoulders, bringing me into the folds of that robe. I wasn't entirely covered like when he had teleported us across the world, but I was inside the warm air within, the air that smelled of something spicy and nice. Not like burned books at all.

"What has happened, Mr. Talbot?" Steph asked. "You smell very strongly of smoke. Did you—?"

"No!" the man said suddenly, cutting him off. "This has nothing to do with that. No, it can't possibly. But the book is safe, I promise you. This, this is a family matter."

"I smell burned pages," I said.

"Yes," the man said, and some of the crazed energy drained out of him. He seemed sad now. Mournful.

"Your bookshop?" Steph asked. His arm tightened around me, as if worried I was about to take an emotional blow.

But the man was shaking his head. "No, no. My apartment."

"Prospero!" Miss Hippolyta burst out.

"It's all right, Miss Hippolyta," he assured her. "I escaped with my life, and nothing was lost that can't be regained." But he was wringing his hands again, almost violently. He saw me noticing this and gave me a steady look with those bloodshot eyes before adding,

"But you were right. Many books were destroyed. Nothing important; they were mostly prosaic novels. An affectation of mine, I admit. No, anything important was in my parents' bookshop. *My* bookshop," he amended with a wince. Then he gave Steph an almost aggressive look. "The tome you are looking for is still quite safe."

"I'm sorry to sound like I'm doubting you, but you found this tome just this morning. Now your apartment has burned down, and many books with it. Are you *sure* this isn't related?" Steph asked.

"No, I don't think it was. I don't think it was. It's not all I found this morning. It's not even the most dangerous. But never mind," Prospero Talbot said, babbling until he ran out of energy to make more words. Then he ran his hands through his matted hair, sending fresh ash from his clothes to fall over the thick pile of the rug below.

"For what it's worth, I did tell him bringing it to you now, under my aegis, was the safest plan," Miss Hippolyta put in. "The longer this object is potentially out in the open, the more dangerous it becomes for all of us."

"I agree," Steph said. "This is why it needs to be in the Tower. It can't fall into the wrong hands. Or even the right hands, given that they will be compelled to destroy it at once."

"That would be a loss," Miss Hippolyta said evenly.

"I know! I know!" Prospero ranted. "Look, it's not a coincidence, the timing of these two things. But they are also not a simple cause and effect, although I can see why you think it might be. More like one cause, two effects."

"Explain," Steph said.

The man nodded as if he had expected that response. Then he collected his thoughts before going on. "I found the book this morning because this morning was the first time I've had the courage to go into my parents' bookshop since they died. *My* bookshop," he corrected himself again, fiercely. But he took a breath and went on. "I found it in the office safe, and I immediately contacted the Wizard. Or tried to. I got you instead."

"I am his apprentice," Steph said, and straightened his spine to stand a bit taller.

"I can vouch for that," Miss Hippolyta said in a mild, but still growly, voice.

"I left the tome in the bookshop, in the safe, with the other things. I went home to grab a late dinner before coming here to meet you, and that's when the fire started," Prospero went on. "Look, I know it sounds crazy, but the fire in my apartment is just a family matter. One I will deal with in due time. But first I want to get rid of this book before anymore attention comes my way. The book and the rest of it." Once again, his voice just trailed off miserably at the end.

"You're sure it wasn't stolen while your apartment was on fire?" Steph asked.

"Positive. I've seen it myself since. It's quite safe," Prospero said. "But I didn't dare take it with me. Just in case he's watching. My brother, I mean."

"So where does that leave us, Mr. Talbot?" Steph asked.

"I'll get it to you, I promise," Prospero said, gesturing earnestly with his smoke-stained hands. "I just need to find a safe way to do that. I'll be in contact. But for now, I really must be going."

"If you need any help—" Steph started to say, but Prospero was already shaking his head.

"No, this is a family matter. I appreciate the offer, but I must speak to my brother myself. I can make him see reason. I'll be in contact as soon as I can."

He didn't wait for any of us to agree. He just faded back into the shadows, then slipped away through the door.

As much as I had told Houdini that I hadn't gained any prognosticating powers, in that moment my mind was in a state of complete certainty.

I was never going to see Prospero Talbot again.

I just hoped the same wasn't true of the book.

CHAPTER

FIVE

My thoughts were all in a whirl. So much so I wasn't really aware of all the steps that brought me back to the kitchen in my uncles' apartment. I was vaguely aware of Steph speaking a few words to Miss Hippolyta, and then a brisk walk back to the mountainside meadow.

Even the experience of teleporting again, an experience I would've sworn would be impossible to tune out the first time I'd done it, was just something that happened to me while I mulled over what had just occurred.

Now I was standing alone in the kitchen, not even certain when Steph had left. Right after bringing me to the bookshop entry, but then he'd had to get back to the Tower straight away. And I had wandered up all those flights of stairs to stare at the makings of a tuna casserole I was far too hungry to wait an hour to eat. I needed something now.

Grilled cheese it was.

My uncle Frank's favorite cast-iron skillet never left the top of his massive chef-quality stove, so all I had to do was shift it to the front burner and start heating it up as I took out some of the bread, cheese and butter I had bought that afternoon.

But as I sliced the bread and cheese to assemble my sandwich, I had to admit that for all the whirling my mind was doing; it wasn't coming up with very many articulate thoughts. I was just... overwhelmed.

"You're making two, right?"

I jumped at the sound of Steph's voice coming from the darkened kitchen doorway. "Don't do that!" I admonished him.

"Sorry. But I did tell you I'd be right back," he said. Then he stepped into the light. He was no longer wearing the multicolored robe over his black clothes, and I had the sudden ridiculous image of that robe plugged in to a magical charger somewhere. Like a cellphone.

I quickly sliced enough more bread and cheese for a second sandwich, then held my open palm over the surface of the cast-iron pan.

Perfect heat.

"I might have missed those exact words," I admitted as I buttered one side of the sandwiches and set them in the pan. I made a minuscule and largely unnecessary adjustment to the burner setting.

"You did look a little dazed. Not that I blame you. I kind of caught you in a flurry of stuff, didn't I?" he said. Then he slid into the little booth tucked into the wall on the opposite side of the tiny kitchen. I thought at first this was just a gesture of keeping out of the way, but then he pulled a thick leather-bound journal out of the front of his tunic and opened it up on the tabletop and started taking various loose notes out from between the pages. By the time he was done, they covered nearly the entire surface.

"What's all that?" I asked.

"This is the enchanted parchment with all of my messages to Prospero Talbot and his responses," he said, nudging the largest of the sheets. "The rest of this is random notes I've been taking while researching in the Wizard's library."

"The Wizard has his own library?" I asked. With far too much enthusiasm. I was already standing in a building that contained more books than I could read in a lifetime.

But I was always hungry for more. It was an addiction. I admit it.

"Your uncles have versions of nearly everything the Wizard has," Steph said. "But the Wizard's editions tend to be earlier—shall we say, differently edited—versions. Most of the differences are superficial, unimportant."

"But not all," I guessed as I peeked at the bottom of the sandwiches before turning them each over to grill the other side. Just the smell of that golden fried bread set my stomach grumbling all over again.

"Not all," he agreed. "Especially when it comes to..." But he trailed off, looking up from his notes to cast his eyes around the room. Then he took out his ebony wand, whispering a few words before balancing the wand on-end in the center of his palm. He sat like that in silence for a moment, his eyes sort of half-shut. Then he gave the upright wand the smallest of tosses, catching it in midair then disappearing it inside his tunic again.

"What was that for?" I asked, looking around the kitchen myself. But everything looked the same as it always did.

"Just making sure we were truly alone, and no one was snooping on us," he said. "We can speak freely here."

"You're sure?" I asked. I caught myself still trying to peer into the corners of the room, as if witches who wanted to spy on us would use anything so obvious as a prosaic recording device.

"Reasonably sure," he allowed. Then he looked down at the tabletop covered in scattered notes. "I usually keep my thoughts neater than this, but I've been too pressed for time to collate everything into my journal. Let me organize this a little to get it out of the way so we can eat."

I turned my back on him to plate up the sandwiches, adding some of the huge homemade pickles I bought by the jar from Juno Wolsey at the Square Pub as well as a generous portion of salt and vinegar chips manufactured in the prosaic world (but so good).

Not the healthiest of meals, but after the events of the evening, I needed a little comfort food.

"Here you go," I said, as I slid Steph's plate in front of him.

"Thanks," he said. He was shuffling notes from one pile to another, but absentmindedly picked up his sandwich to take a bite. Then he had to drop everything to deal with the mouthful of hot cheese he apparently hadn't been expecting.

"I should've mentioned it's still hot," I said, even though touching the bread should've made that obvious.

He mumbled something around that mouthful of food. Then he swallowed and said, "That's amazing. What's in that?"

"Just bread and cheese," I said with a shrug. His eyes narrowed at me chidingly, and I added, "The bread is from LeBeau's bakery. It's his own take on pumpernickel. Isn't it good? And it pairs so well with the gruyere. That's just from a local prosaic dairy that the Abergavennies buy from. Well, local in the sense that their farm is in Wisconsin, but really close to Minnesota. The Dijon mustard is just the usual prosaic brand, but I like it."

"When you throw something together, you really throw something together," he said, and took another, more careful bite from his sandwich.

"Thanks," I said. "I've been experimenting with a few things now that I cook most of my own food. I never did any cooking at all until I came to live here. It was always academy cafeteria food for me. I mean, I still just heat up something from a can far too many nights, but I've been trying to branch out a little."

"That sounds... lovely," he said, and became far too focused on moving his notes around again.

"That's not what you were about to say," I guessed.

"Sorry. I was thinking that it sounded lonely. But you seem so happy here, it didn't seem like the right thing to say," he said with a cautious glance up at me.

"It *is* lonely sometimes," I admitted. "I mean, Houdini is usually here." I was distracted for a moment, wondering just where that little dragon had gone. Was he still in the nook? I'd have to go find him if he didn't turn up soon.

But Steph was still looking at me, waiting for the rest of what I had been saying. "My uncles will be home soon. Then I won't be lonely at all. But aren't *you* lonely? I mean, I know you live with the Wizard, but what's that really like?"

"Well, when he's focused on something that doesn't involve me, like he is just now, it can indeed be a little lonely," he admitted. "But it has allowed me extra time on my own for researching chaos magic, so it's not all bad. Are you ready to hear what I know?"

"Absolutely," I said, and started digging into my own sandwich.

"First of all, the Wizard doesn't have any more texts that deal with the subject than you do here in the Weal and Woe Bookshop," he said. "But, like I said before, sometimes the little differences in his editions matter. In one particular instance, the book itself made no reference to chaos magic, but I got the strong sense that a section that was meant to deal with it had been removed."

"By censors," I guessed.

"Probably," he agreed. "As much as I'd love to know what it said, I can't find an edition of the text anywhere that contains it. And the Wizard and I have put feelers out everywhere."

I felt a stab of disappointment, but clearly he was nowhere near finished bringing me up to date. We had, after all, just gotten back from an expedition to track down something. "What *did* you find?" I asked.

"There was a title listed in the reference index in the back of the book," he said with the faintest hint of a grin. "A reference to an older tome that also dealt with chaos magic, but only in part. In fact, the book in question is technically about binary systems."

"Binary systems? Like, astronomy?" I asked, confused.

"Exactly!" he said, and the grin cranked up a few notches. "An exceedingly dry text about the mathematics of binary systems from the days before the prosaics discovered calculus. I'm no mathematician, but even I can tell this wizard's math is faulty. It's a miracle he knew what a binary system was at all; that took magical amplification on top of the best prosaic telescope around at the time."

"But what does that have to do with chaos magic?" I asked.

"This wizard had some pretty out-there ideas about what two stars in a binary system meant," Steph said. "I'm not talking physics, which he didn't really have a grasp of. No, everything for him was a magical, symbolic thing. But what he was drawn to the most was the idea of splitting all magic into sub-disciplines of either chaos, or of its opposite, order."

"Order magic," I said. "I've never heard of that."

"I thought the same thing when I first read it," Steph said. "Then I realized this crazy old wizard might be on to something. Only in the days between his time and ours, chaos magic has been driven into obscurity."

"And order magic has become so ubiquitous, we no longer even need a word for it," I finished for him.

He blinked as if startled that I had jumped so quickly to that conclusion. Then he reached across the table to squeeze my hand in his.

I tried to ignore how buttery both our hands were.

"Most of what I just told you is just what Prospero Talbot gleaned from a quick scan of the work," Steph said. "He was only looking at it to make sure it was the book the Wizard and I were looking for. All I knew was the title, and that it must contain something. But I don't want to get your hopes up. This tome is over a thousand pages of various iterations of the same math problems imperfectly solved, plus a bare six pages at about the two-thirds point that delineate his thoughts on order and chaos. And he might be wrong about everything."

"Only it makes so much sense," I said.

"That's when you have to be the most careful," Steph said. "The most seductive falsehoods are the ones that just make so much sense."

"I know," I said. "But I can't help thinking of what it could mean if he was right."

"What are you thinking it might mean?" Steph asked.

"Well," I said, and swallowed hard before going on. I was about to say things out loud I'd only been thinking in my head.

But I'd been thinking them a lot lately.

"My mother, her magic feels like it's a thing of chaos. Like mine, but I guess better controlled," I said.

"She's had some training, then," Steph said loyally.

"Maybe," I allowed. "But my uncle Carlo, his magic is very much a thing of order. I've never seen him do anything that felt like it hearkened to any of the common magical fields of study like ritual magic or illusions or potion-making or anything like that. He just... creates order."

"I don't know your uncle as well as you do, but I think that fits what I've seen," he said.

"And they were twins," I said.

"That's news to me," he said. "Interesting. But you don't have any siblings?"

"That's just the thing," I said, swallowing again. This was making me more emotional than it ought to, given that we were discussing basically hypotheticals. "I don't know for sure. I don't remember anything from before my first day at my first magical academy when I was five."

"And your mother never told you anything about your family," he said. Not a question. But I shook my head anyway. "But your gut is telling you something," he went on.

I nodded.

Steph looked down and seemed to only then notice that he was still holding my hand. He let it go to tug at his own lip in thought. "I need to talk to the Wizard about all this. But I can't until his meditations are done. Which is fine. It's only going to be another day or two for that. But what I really need is to get a hold of this book."

He picked up the enchanted parchment, but there was no new writing on it.

"It's so late there. Surely you'll hear something tomorrow," I said.

"Yeah," he said, tucking it away back in his journal. Then he gathered up the other notes, stacking them neatly before tucking them into the pages as well.

He was packing up to go. But I really shouldn't feel sad about that. I was pretty sure this was the longest time the two of us had been in each other's company, ever.

"Tabitha," he said suddenly, just as I had gotten up to clear the plates away. "Tell me what you're sensing. I know you'd probably prefer to say nothing until you know for sure, and I respect that. But tell me anyway."

"I think I must have a sibling, somewhere," I said. "Maybe not a twin, but someone, somewhere."

"Older or younger?" he asked.

I shrugged. "It's just a vague feeling that I'm not alone. But the truth is, I don't know who my father was. I don't know if he's alive or dead, if he had another family before, or if he has one now. There are lots of ways I could have a sibling and not know it. I mean, I see so little of my mother, she could've had another child and I don't think I'd even know."

I brought the plates over to the sink and started running water into the plastic basin I used for washing up. The air filled with the scent of lavender when I added a squirt of soap. My uncles had a favorite scent, there was no question about that. I smiled fondly, but that smile quickly faded.

I wasn't telling Steph everything, and I felt bad about that. But, like he had noted, I wanted to be sure before I started throwing theories around. I mean, speculating about an unknown father was one thing. If I was going to speculate about my actual mother, that was something I was much more reluctant to do.

But I kept what I called a dream journal, a record of all of her visitations to me over the years. I remembered the encounters like dreams, all save the last one, but I had a gut sense that I recalled them all, even if only vaguely.

So I knew for a fact there was a time when I was about ten when I didn't see my mother for an entire year. Plenty of time for her to have a baby without me ever seeing her looking any differently.

Did I have a sibling? Was there a little Greene kid ten years younger than me that was crushing it with order magic? Or did they, unlike my uncle, choose some other discipline?

If they had, they'd be basically invisible. Something I had never had any hope of being, as much as I'd wished for it more than once through my long, chaotic childhood.

"It's late, and I have to get back to the Tower," Steph said, and I looked over my shoulder to see him getting up from the table. "I'll be in touch as soon as I know anything."

"I'd like to come with you to see the book," I said as I rinsed the first of the plates and set it in the drying rack beside the sink. "I'll close the bookshop if I have to. I'll go in the middle of the night. Anything."

"I'll keep that in mind," he said. "Prospero was cagey, but I don't think any of that was about you. I'm sure he'll agree to both of us meeting him." He came over to stand beside me at the sink. The journal was once more out of sight, the same as his wand, and he had both of his hands tucked into his pockets. He could pass for a cat burglar about to head out on a job, save for the paleness of his face. That would be a dead giveaway even in the moonless night we were having.

"He wants to get rid of it quickly, he said. So probably tomorrow?" I said, trying not to hope too much.

"Tomorrow," Steph said with a definite sort of nod.

I could almost swear that he leaned in towards me in that moment, but by the time I had my hands out of the dishwater to reach for the closest towel, he was suddenly three steps away from me. Like he'd teleported backwards just that little bit without so much as a whoosh of wind.

He was mostly in the shadow of the corridor outside the kitchen now, so I couldn't be sure. But I thought he might be blushing in acute embarrassment.

He definitely wasn't meeting my eyes, though.

"Tomorrow," he said again. Then he turned and, in a completely conventional way, headed down the stairs from my uncles' apartment to the top level of the bookshop below.

And now I had another mystery to puzzle over as I finished washing up from our little dinner.

Was I deluding myself, or had he just been about to kiss me?

CHAPTER
SIX

When I finished cleaning up the kitchen, I was more than a little surprised to see it was only eight o'clock. It felt far later than that.

I wondered if there was such a thing as magical teleportation jet lag. I'd have to ask Steph the next time I saw him.

Tomorrow. I'd see him tomorrow. I could ask him then.

I knew I had the world's silliest grin on my face, but I couldn't help it. That little bit of certainty was worth all the rest of my life being a little crazy just now.

I was going to see Steph tomorrow.

But when I cast one last glance around the spotless kitchen, I realized that Houdini's food bowl had spent the entire day untouched.

I hadn't seen him since I had opened the bookshop and he had gone up to the nook to nap.

Turning off the kitchen light, I headed down the apartment hallway, which was diffusely lit from what evening sun made it in through the apartment's north-facing windows to the darkened stairwell that led down to the bookshop below.

The bookshop itself was lit to the same level day or night, a pleasantly warm glow that always seemed to be coming down from just the perfect angle to hit whatever page anyone was reading at the time, but had no visible source. The topmost level was mostly storage, and the smell here was mustier than below from the boxes of prosaic paperbacks that had sat untouched for far too long.

Then I was down in the levels of the bookshop that were given over entirely to a variety of magical texts, and the smells of leather and vellum, parchment and exotic inks closed in around me like an aromatic hug. There was no sound but my own feet on the wooden steps of the staircases that ran back and forth in the heart of the building, a steady beat that was just a little slower than the beat of my anxious heart.

Then I was on the fourth level, the very middle of the bookshop, and I left the stairs behind to head towards the front of the bookshop. The little nook set aside for my own use was clustered around one of the few windows that looked out into the prosaic world. I could see its light ahead of me; it had an unfettered view of the setting sun, especially at this time of the year when the seasonal angle of the planet put that sunset precisely between two of the taller buildings west of the bookshop. It wasn't quite Manhattanhenge, but I had been enjoying it for the last few days.

It would only last for a few days more.

"Houdini?" I called softly as I drew close enough to reach the elongated rectangle of sunlight on the bookshop's hardwood floor.

"Here," he said at once, but miserably.

It certainly looked like he'd been napping, curled up as he was in the window seat where the sunlight was strongest. But looking at the stacks of books left out on the heavy wooden table in the center of the nook, I doubted he'd been napping the entire day.

There were more than a dozen books there, all left open to various pages, still arrayed in random locations over the tabletop. I saw texts in four languages I knew and at least two I didn't.

I also saw a scattering of artistic representations of dragons.

"Houdini, you need to tell me what's bothering you," I said.

"It's nothing, really," he said. But he wasn't remotely convincing.

"Something's upset you, and I want to know what it is," I said. I sat down on the window seat beside him. He uncurled enough to crawl into my lap, careful to be sure his head was conveniently placed under my hand before settling back into his curled-up form. I took the hint and stroked the back of his neck fondly, careful not to touch his ears.

"You do realize that Miss Snooty Cat is no more a cat than I am a dog," he said at last.

"I never really thought about it," I admitted. "Isn't she Barnardo's familiar?"

Houdini sniffed, both in dog form on my lap and telepathically in the back of my mind. "What is this human obsession with familiars?"

"It's more of a witch obsession than a human one, but point taken," I said. "She's his companion, then, as you are mine?"

"Just so," Houdini said.

"But not a cat," I said.

"She is a matagot," Houdini told me.

"Oh, right," I said. I'd heard of those, of course. Most witches had. They were magical creatures generally found in the southern part of France. They usually looked like black cats, but could also look like foxes or rats or other things. It depended on the matagot's preference, from what I'd read.

But what I'd never read was of one who chose the form of a Siamese black cat. That felt awfully specific, and not indigenous to that area.

"She's from here, not from France," Houdini told me. Not for the first time, it felt like he could read my mind, in addition to speaking into it. That was always unsettling. I doubted I would ever get used to it, even though I knew he never meant any harm when he did it.

"I guess it would fit for her personality, wanting to look like an extra fancy kind of cat," I said.

"Her siblings look like alleycats, or so she tells me," Houdini said. "I don't think she even cares that she never sees them. She knows exactly where all of them live, and has a thousand ways to keep in touch with them. She just doesn't."

"I suppose she's like a cat in that way," I said. "We've always known she was exceptionally well named. I almost wonder how Barnardo came up with it, considering how oblivious he seems to her... well, snootiness."

"He didn't name her," Houdini told me. "It was Barnardo's father who named her. She was his companion until he died."

"Oh, dear," I said. "I've heard that can be bad, keeping a matagot tied to you when you're dying. The stories say your death will be long, protracted and painful."

"She wasn't there against her will," he said. "She chose to be there with him, and she has chosen to stay with Barnardo. She wasn't lured to them with food, and she isn't paying them in gold for keeping her."

"That's good, I suppose," I said. But I was also a tiny bit disappointed, since that would've made a good theory for how Barnardo made his money. Keeping Miss Snooty Cat happy. It would explain so much.

"To be honest, she says they are companions, but that's not how she talks about it at all," Houdini said, as if ashamed to admit it out loud. "She thinks of him as her pet. It's rather unseemly. It makes me uncomfortable."

"I can see why," I said. "But somehow I don't think that's why you're so upset today."

"No, I've known about that for some time now," he said with a sigh. "But she's known things for some time, too. Things I never told her."

"She knows you're a dragon?" I asked, trying not to sound alarmed.

"I don't *think* so," he said with extreme precision. "But she definitely knows I am no more a dog than she is a cat. She knows that much. And she has guessed that what I am truly is a source of great mystery to me."

"You know you're a dragon," I said.

"But I don't know what *kind*," he all but wailed in my mind. "I don't know who my family is, or why they lost me, or if they are even looking for me."

"I'm sorry. I haven't helped with any of that as much as I promised to. I've let you down," I said.

"No, you haven't," he said. "You've done your best. I've done my best. Even the bookshop has done its best. But what I need to know isn't in books. And without books, we're a bit at a loss, aren't we?"

"And talking to Miss Snooty Cat upset you because we're at an impasse?" I asked.

"She... said some things," Houdini said darkly. He ducked his head until it was half-buried under my knee.

"What did she say?" I asked.

"She said she could find out what I am," he said. "Whether I wanted her to or not, she could ask around and find out what I am."

"Given the power Agatha put into the spells that protect you, I really doubt she can," I said. "Matagots are powerful, but not that powerful."

I mean, this was Agatha we were talking about. Even after her death, her magic lived on.

And as I touched the collar around Houdini's neck, I remembered all the spells Audrey and I had worked on together to supplement Agatha's own spells. That collar cloaked Houdini from even the most powerful wizard's sight as anything besides the dog Agatha had disguised him as. I had total confidence in my ability to write a spell, even if I knew I could never perform it myself.

And I had even more confidence in Audrey's ability to get more out of the words of my spell than even I had known was possible.

"Barnardo doesn't know what you are," I said, although it was kind of a question.

"No, he's clueless," Houdini said with a sigh. It was really upsetting him, Miss Snooty Cat's attitude to the man who adored her.

"Steph is coming by tomorrow," I told him, and waited a second for my heart to finish flipping over before I went on. "We can ask him to double-check all the spells of protection around you. I'm sure you're safe, but I know you will *feel* safer if Steph tells you that you are."

I didn't mind. Really. Steph wasn't the Wizard's apprentice for no reason. He had tremendous power in his own right. It was perfectly understandable that Houdini looked up to that.

I was just stifling the thought that if we found the tome and unlocked the secrets of chaos magic, that I could be powerful enough for Houdini to look up to me too when I realized that something was still worrying Houdini's mind.

"What is it?" I asked him.

"Would it be terrible if I asked her for help?" he said. Even telepathically, this came out as a low mumble I could barely parse into separate words.

"What do you mean?" I asked him.

He untucked his head and climbed out of my lap to sit beside me, the better to look at me as something close to equals.

"What if I told her what I was, or as much as I know what I am, anyway? What if I trusted her with that secret? Do you think she could help me find my family?"

"Oh, Houdini," I said. "I know how much this means to you, and how much you'd be willing to risk to find your answers. But is Miss Snooty Cat really someone you can trust? Are you sure?"

"No. No, I'm not sure," he said miserably.

"Then I really think you should take all the time you need to decide this. As long as it takes," I said.

"I wish I could," he said, if anything even more miserably than before.

"What do you mean?" I asked.

"She knows how badly I want answers, although she doesn't

know the questions, precisely," he said. "She's given me until tomorrow to ask her for her help. After sunset tomorrow, she vows she will never help me with it again. Not for anything."

"Well, stuff her, then," I said, angry on his behalf.

"But what if she can help?" he pressed.

"If she can help, then there are other ways to get the same answers she can get," I said. "What's she going to do? Ask around? We can do that too."

"Can we?" he asked.

Granted, I didn't know where to start. But I was still pretty sure the answer was yes.

But all I said was, "I don't like how she's pressuring you."

"Oh, it's nothing," Houdini said dismissively. "She likes to manipulate. That's all she's doing. Manipulating. She wants to see me squirm. That's why she's given me a ticking clock. So to speak."

"I still don't like it," I said. "She guesses you need help, but she doesn't know with what. And then she puts a time limit on that help? Just because she's bored?"

"Well, not *just* because she's bored," Houdini said hedgingly.

"What does she want in return?" I asked.

"Just a boon," he said.

"What kind of boon?" I asked.

Dogs can't blush, but he hung his head at an angle that conveyed the same sense of being mildly ashamed.

"A boon to be specified at a later date," he said.

"Nope!" I said, dusting my hands dramatically as if that ended the matter. Because, for me, that would totally end the matter.

"But what if she—" he started to say again.

But I interrupted him at once. "Nope! She's got a very fixed time line but a very vague price? No way. She's not dealing fairly with you."

"I really think this is my decision," he said, sniffing more in a formal sense of offense than hurt feelings. Or, at least, I was pretty sure that was the case.

"It's absolutely your decision," I gave in with a sigh. "Just promise me, before you tell her anything, you get some kind of contract with everything spelled out before you agree to anything. I would prefer you ask Steph for his help. He's very good at magical contracts. But at least some prosaic world boilerplate would do. Anything besides something where she sets all the terms and you have nothing to protect you."

"I will consider your advice," Houdini said, still offended.

"I don't want to tell you your business, but I did swear to protect you when I accepted Agatha's wishes in her will," I reminded him.

"I understand," he said stiffly. But then he relented a little. "If Steph comes tomorrow as you say, then I will speak to him about this. That will fall inside of Miss Snooty Cat's timeline. That will be acceptable to me."

"He said he'd be here," I promised him.

When the two of us finally made our way upstairs to bed, I couldn't help but notice that both of us took quite some time to quiet our brains down enough for sleep.

Tomorrow was going to be a very big day for both of us.

CHAPTER
SEVEN

The next morning, for the first time ever, I missed the usual breakfast meetup in the teashop.

Partly, this was out of solidarity to Houdini, who was still acting very quiet and withdrawn as I got up and got dressed. When I realized he hadn't even moved from the spot on the bed he had occupied all night long, near my knees under the covers, I stopped in the process of putting on my sneakers and threw back the bedding to stroke the short length of his curled up spine.

I didn't say a word, and neither did he. But we came to a silent understanding. He wasn't ready to face Miss Snooty Cat yet, and I wasn't going to go down to breakfast without him.

So we ate alone together in my uncles' kitchen. I had buttered toast and instant coffee, and he had the usual dry kibble. Neither one of us complained, but I didn't think either of us was really satisfied.

But the other reason I had decided not to go down was that I really wanted to talk to Audrey about what happened. Only my chaos magic was like Houdini really being a dragon: it was something Barnardo didn't know about. Unlike Houdini's secret, I was free to share mine if I wanted.

But I really didn't want to.

I had gotten spoiled living in the Square, that was for sure, I mused as I washed my plate and cup and set them in the rack with the dishes from dinner the night before. For all my life, I had been safe in assuming that no one would want to have anything to do with me after a few days of seeing me attempt magic at whatever academy I was currently the new student in. And that assumption had never steered me wrong. I wasn't exactly bullied, or anything like that. No, I was just quietly avoided. Getting to know me better wasn't going to be good for anyone's future prospects.

But since coming to the Square, my lack of magic hadn't come up with anyone. Some of the other residents did magic constantly, like the Trio, now just a Duo. They used all the glamor magic they possessed—which was an impressive amount—daily inside the confines of the Inanna Spa & Salon and even just out walking from point to point around the Square. I doubted I really knew what either Cressida or Cleopatra looked like without their magical illusions up at full force.

But then there were others, like... well, Barnardo. I knew he could use magic, or at least that he possessed magical items. But I had never actually seen him casting a spell.

Most of the rest of the Square fell somewhere in the middle of those two extremes. But the point was, no one judged anyone else for what they did or didn't do.

Except, perhaps, for Barnardo and the Trio, now a Duo. They rather actively reviled each other. But I didn't get the sense that magic was the basis for that beef at all.

It had taken me a little time after moving to the Square to realize that no one was ever going to care how much magic I did or didn't do. And it took even longer before I trusted that fact well enough to let a lifetime of closely held anxiety over being judged and found wanting just go.

But I had. Hence the celebratory feeling I had woken with just the day before. It was amazing living in this place.

I didn't want to do anything to risk that changing. And having people find out that my magic wasn't so much nonexistent as out of control, and actually forbidden by the High Council? That would be the hugest of risks.

As much as I adored Barnardo, I knew full well he was a gossip. His knowing the rumors and having the details on everyone was kind of what made him a valuable part of our little investigating group.

I didn't know how he would feel about me being a chaos witch. But I knew for sure it was safer for me if he didn't know.

So I couldn't talk to Audrey until he had gone.

Unfortunately, that meant waiting until her teashop was open for business. Even a little past it, until after her morning rush had passed. So Houdini and I went down and opened the bookshop early.

At least there was a request in the magic tome. The book that was being searched for wasn't particularly rare, but the customer in question somewhere in China needed ten copies of it. I guessed someone was teaching a class, or perhaps hosting a particularly esoteric book club.

I risked turning on the computer to check our inventory records. Since putting on the silver bracelet that Steph and the Wizard had given me, I no longer shot sparks at random. It was perfectly safe for me to touch the electronics. I only ran an average risk of breaking something.

Well, given my limited knowledge of computers, that was probably a slightly more than average risk. But it was still manageable.

I found we had four copies of the book in question and wrote that response in the tome before heading deep into the stacks to find the physical copies.

As was all too common with the bookshop, especially when my uncle Carlo wasn't there, they weren't all in one place. It took the better part of the morning to track them all down. I actually found the fourth on the table in my nook mixed in with the books Houdini had been pouring over the day before. Houdini himself was napping in the dog bed under the front desk, nominally watching out for customers.

I would have to re-shelve all those dragon books later. And I should probably at least page through them to see if anything useful jumped out at me while I did that. But in the meantime, I wrapped up the four copies I had found, then turned the sign on the door over to *closed*.

"Houdini," I said, poking my head under the desk. He blinked up at me. "I have a package to bring to the pub to make the mail call for the afternoon portal exchange. Then I'm going to head over to the teashop to see Audrey. Do you want to come with?"

"No, thank you," he said, not quite despondently.

"Can I get you anything?"

"No."

"Not even a few of those pumpkin peanut butter treats?" I offered.

"Well, those, certainly," he said, and actually sounded ever so slightly cheered. But then he added, "Do you know *when* we're going to see Steph today?"

"Not exactly. He's waiting to hear from someone else, so it's not really up to him. But I know he's anxious to get this done, so it will be as soon as possible. Okay?" I said.

"Perfectly fine," Houdini said, then put his nose back under his back knee to resume his nap.

This August day was only a shade less perfect than the day before. It was still sunny, but the blue of the sky was starting to look a little hazy. The wildfire smoke was drifting south from Canada again.

You'd think with all the power of the witches of the world, we could do something about it. It was scarcely just a prosaic problem. With very rare exceptions, we all breathed the same air.

But there was nothing *I* could do about it, save to hope for an early winter storm to smother the flames.

The pub had a decent-sized lunchtime crowd, which made me

nervous for my timing at the teashop. I put my package with the others waiting in a cart to be hauled to the portal at the heart of the hedge maze. From the portal, they'd all be teleported to other portals all over the world, but the first and last steps were quite mundane sweat labor.

I went back out into the sun and crossed the Square again to the Loose Leaves Teashop. There were only two customers I could see when I came in through the doors on the Square side of the shop. But the first was just putting her change in her pocket before carrying her travel mug of tea out the prosaic side of the building.

And the second turned out to be Liam, who was, for whatever reason, looking even more despondent than Houdini.

"What's up?" I asked him as I sat across from him at the table where he was nursing a large glass of chai, poking at the ice cubes with a completely superfluous stainless steel straw.

"Oh, hey, Tabitha," he said when he saw me. "You missed breakfast."

"Is breakfast why you're down?" I asked.

"No, I'm fine," he said.

Everything about his body language and his facial expression was saying exactly the opposite.

I sat back in my chair and crossed my arms, giving him my sternest "I don't believe you" look. But all of his attention was focused on those ice cubes. So I finally had to just make a stab in the dark, "I guess your job interviews didn't go as well as you hoped."

"No," he said, then scrunched up his face in thought before saying, "Well, to be fair, I don't think they were ever going to."

"Why's that?" I asked.

"They were kind of random," he said. "I mean, I scanned the online listings and just grabbed whatever seemed interesting. So I guess *I* was kind of random."

"Is that a bad thing?" I asked. "I mean, it's not exactly strange to not know what you want to do with your life at our age."

"Audrey knows," Liam said, dropping his voice and glancing

nervously towards the counter, but Audrey was out of sight. We could hear banging around in the back room, probably Audrey pulling the afternoon's baked goods out of the oven.

"Yeah, and she's good at it. This shop is a perfect fit for her in a lot of ways," I admitted. "But, Liam, four months ago, she didn't know that. She graduated with no real prospects and went back home to her parents. This opportunity just fell into her lap. She's made more than the most of it, but she didn't plan for it."

"Are you trying to make me feel better?" he asked, narrowing his eyes suspiciously at me.

"Of course," I said blithely. "That's what friends do."

"Yeah, but are you trying to make me feel better by saying that at least I'm not back at my parents' house in an anonymous small town in the middle of the prairies of western Minnesota?" he pressed.

"No," I said with a laugh. "First of all, I live with my uncles. That's practically going back home to your parents. Which is some-times a necessary—and not a bad—thing. And second of all, you have five roommates."

"Six now," Liam said with a wince.

"Six?"

"Yeah, Duo, whose name is the one on the lease, has a girlfriend now," he said.

"Six roommates, but still just the two bedrooms," I said.

"Five of us bunk in one, since Duo and his girlfriend need a little privacy," he said. Then he chuckled despite himself and finally took a proper gulp from his now watered-down chai. "Why do you think I'm here all the time?"

"Because of the company?" I said.

"That too," he said, but he was looking past me now, towards the teashop counter. I didn't have to turn in my chair to know that Audrey was in view now. It was written all over Liam's face.

"Tabitha! There you are! We missed you at breakfast," Audrey said as she came out from behind the counter to give me a quick hug.

"Sorry to bail without warning, but Houdini was feeling a little down, so the two of us stayed in. But I really should've sent you a message or something," I mumbled.

"Is Houdini okay?" Audrey asked anxiously.

"Yes, just some Houdini business," I said. "He's facing a big decision I can't really talk about without his permission. But once he's made the correct choice, I'm sure he'll feel better about it all soon."

Or so I hoped. The idea of him owing a boon to the likes of Miss Snooty Cat, and likely not even getting anything worth knowing in return, still turned my stomach.

Audrey slid into the chair next to mine, studying my face with an intensity that nearly had me squirming. Then she said, "There's something else. Bothering you, I mean."

"I had something I was going to tell you, but it can wait," I said. I could see she was about to argue, so I did the one thing that was guaranteed to sidetrack her.

I drew the attention back to Liam.

"I was just thinking, Liam is having a little trouble finding what he needs most," I said. "And as I recall, you had a spell for that."

"Oh, yes," Audrey said, flushing. "That didn't exactly work out last time, you know."

If by "not exactly working out" she meant me blowing all the porcelain in her teashop into smithereens and setting the table centerpieces on fire, I would have to agree. It most definitely hadn't worked out.

But that was before my silver bracelet. I was sure that couldn't happen twice.

Well, I was pretty sure.

"It would probably go more smoothly if I wasn't here," I said.

"Oh, that's not what I meant!" Audrey was quick to say.

"No, I know," I said. "But it was one of your grandaunt Agatha's spells. Her spells tended to have a vibe to them, if that's the right word. You casting the magic and Liam receiving the magic, it makes sense it should be just the two of you."

Liam flushed and stammered but couldn't get out any intelligible words, so he settled for drinking down the last of his chai.

"The spell specifically was for helping a witch find what she was looking for," Audrey said after a moment's thought.

"Yes, but let me take a pass at it. I think I can tweak it to work for Liam," I said.

"You can?" Liam asked with undisguised enthusiasm.

"I can *try*," I stressed, but he was already all but hopping up and down in his seat.

"This is perfect. Just perfect! All I need is some kind of guidance towards the right job," he said. "With the right job, I know I can work hard enough to get a place of my own before Duo starts pushing us all out the door."

"You think that's likely to happen?" Audrey asked, alarmed.

"If the girlfriend sticks around, sure. And if having five guys sharing the apartment with her and Duo hasn't driven her away yet, I don't know what could," Liam said. But for once, he didn't sound glum about his own future prospects.

"I should get back to the bookshop," I said, getting up from the table.

"So soon?" Audrey asked.

"I don't want to leave Houdini alone today," I said. "And besides, Steph is supposed to be coming to see me at some point. I'd really hate to miss him."

Not that he couldn't find me, the teashop being exactly the second place he was bound to look for me.

"I should dig out that spell for you to look at before you go," Audrey said, and turned towards the office behind the counter.

"No, remember, I have copies of all of Agatha's books in my nook in the bookshop," I reminded her. "It's been slow in the bookshop. I'm sure I'll have plenty of time to dig into it this afternoon."

"At least until Steph interrupts you," Audrey said, but I could tell from the glint in her eyes that she was only teasing.

But Liam grasped both of my hands in his and squeezed them

almost too tightly. "I can't tell you how much I appreciate this, Tabitha," he said.

"Maybe wait until you see if the spell helps before you thank me," I said.

"Oh, it will. I know it will. With your research and Audrey's skills, they always work, don't they?" he said, grinning. "But either way, honestly, thanks for even trying to help me out."

"Of course," I said. I almost had to wipe a tear away at the earnestness of his tone as he said those words. But I knew where they were coming from. Wasn't I also wrestling with the new feelings of knowing the people around me were there to support me no matter what? Liam was feeling that, too.

I just hoped I could avoid disappointing him.

Well, if worst came to worst, I could always convince my uncles to hire him to work in the bookshop.

But after getting back to that bookshop and opening the door to a complete lack of customers, I went back to hoping the spell worked out. Because once my uncles were back in town, I wasn't sure how much longer *I* would be employed, let alone Liam.

I didn't want to be unemployed. But I really didn't want to leave the Square.

CHAPTER

EIGHT

The minutes felt like hours. I hated waiting. My whole life, I had always hated waiting. But this waiting was filled with so many worried thoughts running in pointless circles through my mind, I didn't have the focus to distract myself with books.

And that had never happened before.

Eventually six o'clock rolled around once more and I got up from my stool behind the apothecary desk to turn the sign to *closed* and lock the front door.

This time, what I sensed behind me wasn't a change in the air. It was the more conventional sound of footsteps coming down the main staircase. I turned to see Steph descending into view, hands in his pockets as he came down the stairs in a skipping beat.

He wasn't wearing his rainbow-colored robe, but I firmly told myself that didn't necessarily mean that there was no news or bad news.

Still, I didn't wait for him even to get to the bottom step before asking, "What happened? Where were you all day? Did you hear anything or not?"

Those words probably came out too fast and too loud, and he pulled his hands out of his pockets to raise them in mock surrender. "Sorry, Tabitha. I was just upstairs talking with Houdini. As pressing as our matter is, his deadline fell sooner."

"You knew about his thing with Miss Snooty Cat?" I asked.

"He told me he wanted to speak to me about something urgent," Steph said.

"How?" I asked.

"You know," he said, and touched the back of his head. "The usual way he does."

"He can do that over distances?" I asked.

"You can too, or have you already forgotten?"

Forgotten when I had called out for Steph with so much magical force I had been heard by every magical being in the Midwest? Or so my friends had told me later. I had also been yelling his name with enough force to blow out my vocal cords for days, so I had no reason to doubt that my mental voice had been just as overdone.

In my defense, I had been fighting for my life at the time.

But the point was, he had heard me. Just like he promised me he would.

Sure, it felt a little less special, knowing that the same thing worked with Houdini as it did between the two of us.

"But I've finished my conversation with Houdini, and the two of us are also under a deadline. Are you ready to head out?" he asked, glancing at a wrist which bore no watch.

"Yeah, but where are we going?" I asked.

"We need to catch the portal stream this time," he said, waving for me to follow him into the Square. "I've told Houdini where we're going, so no worries there. He says he'll see you when you're back and catch you up on his decision."

"What *was* his decision?" I asked as we fast-walked out of the bookshop's backdoor and into the hedge maze.

"I don't know, actually. He has a little time yet, and is still weighing his options," he said.

"I hope you told him not to take her up on it," I said, but he, maddeningly, said nothing. "Steph? Did you tell him to do it?"

"I didn't advise him either way," Steph said. "But what details of our conversation you will be privy to is up to Houdini when he's ready to talk to you. Sorry," he added, sounding genuinely contrite.

"No, that's fair," I grudgingly admitted. "It's his decision and his business. As much as I'd like to keep him safe by making decisions *for* him."

"He heard what you said to him. You can trust in that," he said.

I looked up at the sky. There were still hours to go before sunset, but I wasn't sure how long our little mission would take. As much as I wanted to see that book and hopefully learn something useful about my power, I really felt bad that I was possibly going to miss being there for Houdini at his big moment.

We reached the open clearing in the heart of the hedge maze, where two curved pillars of stone stood, looking for all the world like they'd been there since the beginning of time. Next to those stones was stacked an assortment of boxes, sacks, and packages. Two young boys I knew by sight from around the Square but not by name sat atop one of the boxes, chatting together and banging the heels of their swinging legs against the box.

Steph and I circled around until we were standing before the stone pillars, one on our left and the other on our right. They were twice as tall as they were apart from each other, and they didn't quite touch at the top, forming instead a sort of broken archway.

But even as I looked at it, the view of the hedges on the far side through the center of that archway started to shimmer. The boys hopped off the box, and each picked up a sack, then stood waiting as the shimmer inside the archway grew brighter even as it started to swirl. The swirling picked up momentum. Then the heart of the cyclone pattern seemed to pull away from us, forming a long tunnel of light.

With no word between them, both of the boys started tossing the stack of packages into the tunnel. Steph and I waited until their flurry of activity slowed down as they reached the heavier items at the bottom of the stack. The two of them together bent to pick up a crate, just barely able to lift it off the ground.

I admit I was apprehensive, looking at that portal. I had travelled through portals before, many times. But I had never gotten used to it.

"Come on," Steph said, his hand closing over my wrist. Before I could even respond, he tugged me with him into the portal.

And my whole world became a swirling rainbow of light. There was a high-pitched hum, but not an unpleasant one, and I could smell something like petrichor in the air.

All of that only lasted a single flash of a moment, and then we were out on the other side. I once more found myself in the middle of the night with mountains blotting the stars by the horizon all around me.

But this was no mountain village we were in now. It was a city. And we were standing on a rooftop garden atop a building. I could see streetlights below us, and I guessed we were only about six floors up. Maybe an office building or an apartment building.

I could hear the sounds of urban life all around us, the voices of patrons moving in and out of restaurants and bars nearby but just out of sight, and the more distant sounds of cars and car horns.

One of those restaurants was frying potatoes, and my mouth instantly began to water.

I had to stop making these expeditions on an empty stomach. Or at least bring a protein bar with me.

"I've never been here before," I said as I looked around the garden. It wasn't as impressive as the hedge maze at the heart of the Square, but the evergreen trees that grew in massive containers all around us screened the portal from prosaic view well enough.

It helped that this particular portal looked like a garden feature, the sort of trellis that should have roses growing all over it. But I didn't think the constant magical use of the structure would allow for anything to grow on it. Once the portal had closed and the last of the shimmer had faded away, it actually looked a little sad.

"We're on the outskirts of Geneva," Steph said.

"I've been to Geneva before, but more the downtown area," I said. Surprisingly, I had never attended an academy here, but I had visited a few magical museums and its prestigious magical library on various school trips.

"Our destination is a little further out, but this was the closest portal," Steph said. "Come on."

I followed him to the door that led into the building, then down flight after flight of stairs until we reached street level.

Then we were out with the bar crowd on the sidewalks. We were too far out from the city for there to be many tourists, and being a Thursday, even the locals weren't out in strong numbers, but it was enough for us to blend in if we needed the cover.

"It's four blocks this way," Steph said, pointing straight ahead of us.

I was mostly distracted by the momentary sight of him with a modern cellphone in his hand, consulting a map. I didn't think he ever used prosaic technology. Then he tucked it away in his pocket, and I realized his Hamlet leggings had just the kind of pocket on the side of the thigh that was meant to store cellphones.

Had that always been there?

"What is it?" Steph asked, pulling me out of my reverie.

"I was just wondering... he said he had the book, right? This is the trip where we finally get to see it?" I said.

"That's what he said."

"And we're sure it's safe?"

I meant the book, but Steph must've thought I meant the situation. He said, "I got more details out of him today about what happened yesterday, and it all tracks. I even confirmed the details I could."

"Like what?" I asked.

"His parents died recently, and suddenly," Steph said. "They were traveling together by car through the prosaic world and had an accident out on a remote road. By the time they were found by the prosaic first responders, they were both gone. No one knows quite what happened, but from what I read online, it's assumed they swerved to avoid something in the road and lost control of the car. It was a mountainous road."

"That's terrible," I said. "So that's why he kept correcting himself about the bookshop."

"You noticed that too? Yes, he inherited the entire establishment. But he left it closed for two weeks after their death. He just couldn't face going in, even though he's worked there since he was a teenager," Steph said.

"No, I'm sure it's filled with memories of his parents," I said.

"Yes, that's what he said," Steph said. "And like he told us, he went in for the first time yesterday to get ready to reopen the shop. But that's when he unlocked the office where his father's private collection of books were stored, a place he was never allowed to go into, not even when he became the assistant manager and often ran the place alone when his parents were away."

"That's when he found the book," I guessed.

"Exactly," Steph said. We had walked two of the four blocks, but had to stop now to wait for a traffic light to change. Not that there were any cars around. We had even left the restaurant traffic behind a block before. The buildings around us now looked like offices and warehouses, all buttoned up and quiet at this hour.

The wind was blowing up the street from behind us, carrying that fried potato smell with it. And I was still hungry.

But occasionally the wind would shift. Only for the briefest of moments, but there was another smell from that other direction, one I could almost place before it was gone again and I was back in the world of golden fried potatoes I could almost taste.

"And the family matter?" I asked as the light changed and we started walking again.

"His brother," Steph said. "He was vaguer about that, but as it didn't pertain to the book, I didn't press. But I gather he, Prospero, alone inherited that bookshop. His brother wasn't given any part of the ownership."

"So his brother set Prospero's apartment on fire?" I asked, incredulous.

Steph just shrugged. "I don't know the specifics, but that's what it sounds like. Family drama. Some families are more into it than others."

"Yeah," I said, but in a low voice. I wasn't sure where my own family fell on the spectrum of loving drama. I mean, I didn't even know who my father was, or whether my hunch about having a younger sibling was even correct. So did that count as high drama, or no drama?

I glanced over at Steph as he looked up and down the last street we had to cross before reaching our destination. I suspected his family was firmly on the no drama side. I knew he had chosen a magical discipline that neither of his parents had shared, but they had been totally supportive of his choosing his own path.

Of course, choosing to pursue the most demanding of magics— ritual magic—and then graduating top of your class with your choice of apprenticeships was usually something even high drama parents could get behind. But still. He felt too self-assured and well-adjusted to not have cool parents.

I was still studying his face in profile when the wind shifted again. This flash of a momentary smell was no longer than the others, but this time I placed it at once.

Smoke. Fire.

Burning books.

"Steph?" I said, but he had smelled it too. We both started running, down the last half of a block to a narrow alleyway between two modest office buildings.

I saw no sign of a magical building lurking at the end of that alley, but only because it was already filled with smoke.

"Stay here!" Steph said, then sprinted down the alleyway.

There was no way I was following that order. I sprinted straight after him.

And kind of regretted it right away. The smoke tore at my lungs, and the heat was intense long before I got my first glimpse of the flames. I felt the icy coldness of a magical barrier, a brief respite from the heat, but I was on the other side before I'd even realized what I was passing through.

Then I could see it: a building that looked for all the world like a Gothic church complete with stained glass windows, only with no religious iconography to be seen anywhere. The heavy wooden doors were smoldering, sending out billows of black smoke even as they started to sag away from the iron hinges.

There was no way we were getting in through those doors. The merest touch was sure to kick up the slow smolder to open flame, and letting fresh air into the interior of that stone building felt like a huge mistake.

Steph was standing dumbstruck just inside the barrier and looked over at me as I stumbled to a halt beside him. I expected him to yell at me for disobeying his order, but he only said, "This way!" and ran down the narrow gap between the stone wall of the Gothic building and the brick wall of the office building in the prosaic world beside it.

What were the locals even going to make of this? Smoke coming from nowhere?

But maybe it wouldn't matter. It certainly looked like they were about to have open flames themselves, if the magical authorities didn't arrive to put out the fire soon.

Steph was already out of sight down that alley, but I hesitated. It was very narrow, extremely hot, and filled with so much smoke I doubted it would be possible to breathe, let alone see once I was inside that space. Steph hadn't thought twice about sprinting in there, but Steph had quick access to all sorts of magic I could only dream about doing.

Highly detailed dreams where I knew every motion and every

archaic phrase to cast the spells with perfect precision, sure, but dreams all the same.

I had never felt less useful in my life.

But I pulled up the neck of my T-shirt to cover my mouth and maybe filter out the smoke, for what little good that would do, and plunged in after him.

I was safer with him than without him. I knew that in my bones.

Even if "with him" was in the heart of a conflagration.

NINE

It took everything I had to keep my eyes open, and even then they weren't worth much. Everything was a watery blur from their constant tearing, and when I blinked them clear, there was still nothing to see but billows of black smoke. And on top of that, the T-shirt was doing nothing. My lungs felt like I was trying to breathe hot ash. Probably because I was trying to breathe air that was full of hot ash. Go figure.

This had been such a mistake.

Then I saw something: a bright flash of magical light about ten feet in front of me, briefly outlining the shape of Steph's silhouette as he used his ebony wand to blow a hole into the stone wall of the Gothic building.

I stumbled forward to see what he had actually done was blow a side door off its hinges, but I was still pretty impressed. I doubted I would've even seen the door in all the smoke.

Not that there was any less smoke where we were. I tried again to blink my eyes clear, but there was some kind of grit in them now, and blinking actually *hurt*.

I felt Steph's hand closing over my wrist and let him guide me away from the blasted door and further inside the building.

Into my own personal hell. All I could see were flames, great pillars of flames that rose up so tall they were licking at the crossbeams that held up the roof far above us. But I knew why those flames appeared to be roaring in neat rows.

They were bookcases. Bookcases once full of books. And they were all dying. I could practically hear them calling out to me as they were consumed by the fire, quickly becoming the very ash that was already making my eyes gush tears.

"This way," Steph said over the roar of the flames. This time he put an arm around my shoulders to steer me away from the horrific sight I couldn't tear my eyes away from.

And into a backroom that was, as yet, untouched by fire. It was filled with smoke—thick, black clouds of smoke—and I knew the books that filled the shelves here would smell of smoke for the rest of their existence. Which would probably be short enough, if the authorities didn't arrive soon with the right sort of magic to put out these fires.

But my eyes skimmed over those shelves of books, drawn to the body that was sprawled across the floor.

I knew that thatch of hair. Even the clothes were the same, although likely more smoke-scented than ever now. It was Prospero Talbot.

And judging from the knife between his shoulder blades, it wasn't the fire that had killed him.

Steph rushed to kneel at his side. I tried to say that it was useless. He was clearly long-since dead given the dark stickiness of the blood congealed in a pool beneath him. But all I could get out was a harsh, racking cough.

But Steph wasn't trying to revive him. He was pulling up the edge of the carpet beneath him. I drew closer and saw that the carpet under the body had been pulled back and folded double before Prospero had fallen over it. And as Steph drew the corner aside, I saw why.

There was a safe built into the floor, flush with the floorboards. I could see the outline of the door in the heavy fireproof metal, but there was no way to open it. There didn't even appear to be any way to lock it: no dial or keyhole or anything.

But that was hardly surprising. It was, after all, a magic safe.

Steph took out his wand again. I stepped back, expecting another blast of magical force, but Steph worked with more finesse than I would have. He just tapped the top of the safe, and the door swung easily open.

But there was nothing inside.

Had the book been there? And where was it now?

I looked around the floor, then at the shelves that lined every wall of the room that appeared to be a sort of office. But, being a bookshop office, there were a lot of books.

A *lot* of books.

"It isn't here," Steph said.

"It could be," I said, and started to move towards the nearest shelf of books. I couldn't remember the title of the book, if Steph had even ever told it to me, but I was pretty sure I'd know it if I saw it.

I'd have to move an array of knick-knacks to see the spines clearly. A brass orrery, a bamboo abacus, and was that a solid gold joy buzzer?

But Steph was pulling on my arm again. "It definitely isn't here. And we have to go. Now."

Then he pointed up, and I tipped my head back to see the rafters overhead were in full flame now, and starting to crack. That roof was coming down, and soon.

I turned away from the bookshelf with a pang in my heart, but the door we had come in from was now impassable. Nothing but a wall of flames that were starting to lick inside the doorway, reaching for the closest books within.

"You have to teleport us out of here," I said.

Steph flinched at my words, and I remembered too late that he didn't have his rainbow-colored robe on. Could he teleport without it? My knowledge of displacement magic was slight—it definitely wasn't something you wanted to mess with if you had as little control over your power as I did—but I knew it was possible for very high level wizards to do it at will.

The Wizard was definitely that kind of high-level doer of magic.

But was Steph?

I mean, in an emergency, could he pull it off?

I don't know what emotions my face was conveying as I thought those thoughts, but they seemed to cause Steph actual pain. He wrenched his gaze away from me and turned to face the back wall of the office.

One of the rafters overhead made a loud cracking sound, and I threw both my arms over my head. But after the longest five seconds of my life, nothing came down on me but a shower of sparks. Painful, but not the end for me.

Yet.

Then I heard the sound of Steph coughing almost uncontrollably. He had his wand in his hand but was doubled over, unable to draw a breath.

Whatever spell he was trying to cast, it needed a verbal as well as a wand gesture component. Well, most spells did, frankly. But in this smoke-filled air, that was a real problem.

I looked down at my own hands, and at the gleam of the silver bracelet around my wrist. I was really good at causing fires. And I had summoned lightning once. But could I do rain? Was a sudden cloudburst chaotic enough for my wonky magic?

I closed my hands into fists, then squeezed my eyes shut as well.

I felt the charm inside the bracelet brushing against my mind. It spoke to me, but not in words like Houdini. It was more like a feeling. A request.

Did I want access to my power?

Yes, please!

I felt two concussive blasts in quick succession. The first was coming from across the room, a blast of hot air washing over me even as I heard the distinctive rattle of stone blocks blowing away from the room, out into the space behind the building. Steph had managed to get his spell out.

But the second came fast after the first, so fast they were nearly simultaneous. And that one came out of me. I suppose if I had managed to direct that power to blast straight ahead, I would've been blown backwards into the burning wall behind me. But since it went in all directions at once, I had no direction for Newton's equal and opposite rule to take me in.

Except straight in. Which it did. It was like I had just imploded my own body. I found myself sprawled on the floor with the wind painfully knocked out of me, my ears ringing loudly, and the air around me suddenly feeling too thick. Like I was underwater.

Steph pulled me to my feet and hustled me out the back of the building even as I felt the first drops of water raining down on me. They were too hot, singeing my bare skin wherever they touched, but still blessedly welcome.

But even as disoriented as I was, it felt like that rain was coming at a funny angle.

And then I was out in the open space of another Geneva alleyway, this one clear of smoke, and that rain just stopped.

"What happened?" I asked, and Steph gestured madly for me to keep my voice down. I didn't have to ask why. Everything still sounded like I was underwater, where I could hear anything at all past the ringing of my ears, and I had a pretty good idea that I wasn't so much speaking as shouting.

And clearly, Steph still wanted us to hurry. He had his arm around me, but which of us needed the support more was an open question. I slipped an arm around him as well, and the two of us staggered out into the street proper.

I thought I heard sirens behind us, but when I tried to look, I couldn't see anything. Not even the flames. I might have seen smoke rising up into the starry night, but even that I wasn't entirely sure about.

But Steph's arm around my shoulders was urging me to hurry, and I followed his lead, hustling along the sidewalk back the way we had come if a block to one side.

Then all at once we weren't hurrying anymore. We were at a dead stop. And I looked up to see the red color of a Don't Walk light. There wasn't a car in sight, or even another pedestrian. But there we were all the same, not walking.

"What did you do?" Steph asked, although it took a real effort for my brain to pick out the words in the garble of sounds that eked into my ears.

"Made it rain?" I said, with an extra attempt to speak softly. But from Steph's wince, I gather I wasn't entirely successful.

"That was from the fire engines," Steph said. "The *prosaic* fire engines."

"They put out the fire?" I said, but when I turned to look back, it was only to see that the buildings between us and what we were fleeing were too tall. I couldn't see a thing.

"They're working on it," Steph said. Then the light changed and we were walking again, if in less of a rush than before.

"How can they? I mean, if their buildings caught fire too, they could do that. But the bookshop is in protected magic space," I said.

"It *was*," he said. Then he looked over at me with the faintest hint of a grin in the twist of his mouth.

"What do you mean?" I asked.

"I don't know for sure, but I felt something shift when you did your little power blast," he said. "You didn't summon rain, obviously." And he pointed with his chin up at the sky above us. The sky without a cloud between us and all the stars. "But I think you did manage to take down all the protective magics that kept the bookshop safely out of the prosaics' awareness."

"Oh, no," I said, my heart sinking. But then I had another thought. "Maybe that's a good thing? I mean, once they could see it, they started putting the fire out. And our authorities still weren't there at all."

"Which seems like another problem entirely, but setting that aside for now," he said with a sigh. Then he pulled me to a halt and turned me to face him.

We were both covered in sooty smoke. Given his all-black outfit, Steph in particular looked like he was geared up for a heist or a covert op of some variety. I just choked back a laugh, which was a good thing, since the expression on his face in that moment was gravely serious.

"Do you know what that means? What you did?" he asked.

He was whispering, but some of my hearing was starting to come back. And apparently I was better than I thought at reading lips.

"No," I said. But mostly because I really didn't want to know.

But since I hadn't said that part out loud, he went ahead and told me. "Those wards have been up for more than a millennium. And they are constantly replenished by the most powerful of wizards. But I know you know this."

"Yes, I know that," I said. He didn't need to say the rest. I knew what he was getting at.

I had just done something that should be impossible. I mean, a team of those top wizards working together might be able to pull it off, but a single witch alone? No way.

And yet I had.

"We need to get out of here, now," Steph said, and I didn't even waste the breath agreeing. I just started back to the portal at a jog. And Steph ran to catch up.

I didn't even slow when I reached all those stairs up to the rooftop garden. But I had to stop when I reached the portal. Because I had no idea what to do from there. Even if there had been a sched-uled opening, I didn't have the power to jump through it on my own.

Steph stopped beside me, digging a hand into his side as if hoping to relieve a stitch there, and looked up at the empty trellis as he fought to get his breath back.

"You couldn't teleport before," I said.

"Not without drawing attention," he said. Then he gave me a dry grin. "If I'd known what you were planning, I might not have been so discreet."

"I wouldn't call what I did *planned*," I said. But I was still too eager to get out of Geneva to join him in finding the humor of the moment. I nodded my head towards the trellis. "Can you do this?"

"Yeah," he said, taking out his wand. But he was still breathing too hard for the focus of spellwork, so he just kept it in his hand as he bent over his knees like a sprinter who's just finished walking it off. He managed to say in a reasonably steady voice, "The book was gone."

"You said." I still wasn't convinced we'd done enough to look for it, but it was pointless to argue now.

"It was," Steph insisted. "Prospero was keeping it in that safe, the one that was completely empty. And it wasn't the only thing meant to be in there. But it was also large." He used his hands to measure out a square somewhat larger than a standard LP. Not ridiculously huge for a book, but definitely larger than any of the books I had seen on the shelves in the office.

Not that I had gotten anything like a good enough look at those.

"I wish I could feel as sure about that as you do," I said. "But I guess I'll have to get used to the idea that it's gone."

"Oh, it's not *gone*," Steph said. I gave him a questioning look, and he went on. "Whoever killed Prospero took what was in the safe and then set fire to the bookshop. It only makes sense."

"His brother?" I asked.

"That's certainly the first place I'm going to look," Steph said.

"Now?" I asked.

"No, we need to get home first," he said. Then he straightened up, giving his wand a little spin through his fingers. An unnecessary flourish.

"So, we have an alibi?" I said.

"No," he drawled. "No, anyone who checks the records will know we were here. There is no point in trying to lie about being in Geneva. But we don't have to have been anywhere near the shop. There are other places nearby. Places I've been to before, doing the Wizard's business. So, yeah, they'll check the records when they start investigating the murder. But by the time anyone thinks to do that, the Wizard will have a cover story for us."

"He will?" I asked. I knew I sounded disbelieving, but I was still getting used to the supportive community thing. I mean, I hadn't even met the Wizard yet. And he'd done so much for me already. Me, basically a stranger who lived near the Tower that he never, to my knowledge, actually came out of.

But, "Yeah," Steph said again. Then he was smiling at me again. Not a dry, gallows humor grin, but a proper smile. "It's far past time, and there's no getting around it now, anyway. It's time for you to meet the Wizard."

"Okay," I said, not sure I understood what all the smiling was about. If the Wizard was truly trying to help me hide the existence of my chaos magic, I had just made his job nearly impossible by what had happened that night.

Then Steph's arm was sliding around me. It took me a confused minute to work out why he was doing this when he hadn't even cast the spell to open the portal, and anyway, how were we supposed to jump through together if he was holding me like that, face to face?

But then I knew. Like half a second before his lips met mine.

Oh. Right. Sometimes people hold on to each other for reasons *besides* fleeing from death and destruction.

And, honestly? I preferred this face-to-face kind of holding.

Even if I knew that the death and destruction were still coming. For a minute, or a couple of minutes, it didn't matter.

CHAPTER

TEN

As it wasn't a scheduled flow time through the portal, Steph had to use his magic to summon a smaller flow of magic just for the two of us. And I experienced my third different teleportation method in two days. This was like the last trip through the portal, but tighter somehow. Like the tunnel of light around us was about to collapse and crush us. Even the sensation of music around us was shriller, almost as if trying to warn us we were about to be smooshed.

Luckily, it was over quickly. But I found myself once more hunched over with my hands on my knees, fighting to get my breath back.

"Sorry," Steph said as he did the same beside me. "I'm not used to doing so much intense magic in such a short period of time. Blasting down two doors, general warding so that the prosaic people of Geneva wouldn't look twice at us, then jumping through that portal at an off-time. I'm a little out of shape."

"I doubt that's true," I said. "You look like you're in top form to me."

He grinned at me, but that grin quickly faded as his face grew more pensive.

"What is it?" I asked him. We were alone at the heart of the hedge maze, and as startling as it was to be back in sunlight after spending the better part of an hour in the middle of the night, it wasn't exactly alarming to see it was still day in Minnesota.

"I have to go," he said.

"But you said we were going to the Wizard," I said.

"I said it was time for you to meet him, but not right this minute," he said. "I have to talk to him first. And he'll probably want to do some preparatory stuff before meeting you. I'm sorry. I didn't mean to mislead you. But I didn't mean it would be straight away."

"No, I can see how that's probably what you meant," I said grudgingly.

"Hey," he said, pulling me closer again. "I got you back here before sunset. There's still time for you to be there with Houdini at the appointed hour."

"If he wants me there," I said. I hoped I didn't sound as sullen as I felt. I kind of wished I was five again and could give in to the urge to pout. Sadly, I was a grownup.

But then Steph kissed me again, and I remembered there were a few upsides to being a grownup.

"I *do* have to go," he said. Which would have been more convincing if he hadn't sandwiched it between kisses.

"You should," I agreed. "The book is out there. We need to get after it before it's really lost."

"You're right," he said with a sigh. Then he gave me a look of such longing it nearly had me changing my mind.

But I really needed to see what was in that book.

He squeezed both of my shoulders and pushed himself back from me like he needed the distance to think clearly. "I'll be back as soon as I can, but I don't know how soon that will be," he said.

"I know," I said. Because that was kind of the defining rule of our relationship.

But that thought was nearly enough to trigger a squee. We had a *relationship*! Luckily, I kept that squee on the inside.

Steph gave me one last nod, then just popped out of existence.

Leaving me to make my own way out of the hedge maze. But when I saw the light was still on in the teashop, I headed there rather than to the bookshop. The teashop or Barnardo's apartment seemed the most logical places for Houdini to have agreed to meet Miss Snooty Cat at sunset, and the teashop was closer. I could check there first.

Having convinced myself I was totally not going in that direction, just in the hope of grabbing a minute or two with my best friend, I jogged through the orchard of fruit trees that grew alongside the hedge maze and towards the tiled patio outside the teashop.

I saw Audrey on the other side of the glass door, just about to lock it for the night. Her face lit up when she saw me, but only briefly. There was deep concern etched all around her eyes as she held the door open for me.

"What happened?" she asked at once.

For a moment, I was totally disoriented. My first thought was that she could somehow just tell that Steph and I had been kissing each other in two cities in the last ten minutes. Which made the worried concern a little strange.

Then I saw Liam standing behind her with nearly the same expression on his face, and it finally dawned on me that I was a bit of a mess. I mean, I looked like I had been crawling through piles of ash and rubble while hot cinders burned little holes in my clothes and smoke permeated into all my pores, because I, in fact, had.

"I'm okay," I told both of them. "Sorry I'm a mess. I wanted to see you right away, but maybe I should shower and change first?"

I really didn't want to mess up Audrey's spotlessly white decor, but I could see I was leaving ashy footprints behind me. If I sat in one of the chairs, or touched the tables, I would undo even more of her cleaning work.

But Audrey just took out her wand and whispered a few arcane words. A soft breeze blew all around me, and I looked down to see I was perfectly clean. I mean, my clothes still had burn holes in them. It wasn't a mending spell. But the smoke smell was out of the fabric and my hair too, and my shoes looked like they might just be salvageable. Which they totally hadn't the second before.

"Nice spell," I said with a thankful smile. I remembered putting it together for her weeks before, one of many parts of my apology for destroying her teashop not once but twice before I learned to control my chaotic outbursts of power.

"It *is* handy, isn't it?" she said with an echoing smile. But the worried looked dropped back down far too soon. "What happened, Tabitha?"

"I'll make a pot of tea," Liam said, and hustled behind the counter to do so. But I could see that even as he worked, he was still listening for what I would say.

"There was a fire," I said. "Obviously. And we didn't get the book."

"The book?" Audrey said.

"Oh, yeah. I was going to tell you about that, but I couldn't do it when Barnardo was here," I said.

"Do you want me to go?" Liam asked from behind the counter.

"No, you already know some of it, about my magic. And anyway, I know with the oath spell you swore to Steph that you couldn't tell anyone about me, even if you wanted to. And why would you want to?" I said.

"I think I now understand even less than before you started to explain," he said with a dry chuckle.

So while the water boiled and then while the tea steeped, I first gave Liam a very short explanation of chaos magic and then explained to both of them about the book and what Steph and I had hoped to find in it.

I had a mug of herbal tea that tasted of almonds and cardamom in my hands as I finally told the tale of all that had happened in Geneva. It was really good tea, but I couldn't help feeling like something hot in my hands shouldn't feel so soothing in the middle of August.

And yet it did.

I skipped over the kissing parts. That was too new of a thing for me. I wanted more time to have it be something special and private, just between Steph and me. For now.

When I had finished talking, we all sat silently for a long stretch of time. Outside the teashop, we could hear the sounds of the night-time insects and varieties of tree frogs that thrived inside the hedge maze, a steady drone of comforting noise.

Then I heard something else, a scratch of dog nails on a stainless steel doorframe. I turned to see Houdini pawing at the door to the Square.

"I'll let him in," Audrey said as she got up from the table. Grateful not to have to get up—sitting felt really good after all that running in Geneva—I just leaned forward to grab the teapot and pour myself a second cup of the almond and cardamom tea.

Beside me, Liam had his phone in his hands, his thumbs racing over the screen nimbly as he typed.

"What are you looking for?" I asked, sitting back just in time as Houdini made one of his leaps without looking into my lap. He always just assumed he would have a safe landing zone, that I wasn't about to get up or hadn't put something obstructive on my lap already.

"News from Geneva," Liam said as he frowned at his screen, then started scrolling down. Houdini bumped his head against my hand, and I stroked his fur, careful not to touch his ears.

"I didn't even think to check," I said. "What does it say?"

"Not much," he said. "And everyone seems to be reprinting the same brief paragraph from the official response from the city. Basically, an abandoned building burned down to the ground, nothing left to salvage, but the fire was stopped before it did more than cosmetic damage to the neighboring structures."

"That bookshop was like a Gothic church," I said. "Not so big as a cathedral, but still. Big."

"Well, it's all gone now," Liam said. Then he looked up at me, his blue eyes steady. "No word of a body. It was still there when you left?"

"Yes," I said. "I know it was. But the roof was starting to come down. Maybe they just haven't found it yet."

"No, there's really nothing left but ash," he said, and scrolled back up to some of the articles he had already scanned. "I can see pictures of the alleys that led to it. There's even an aerial photo of a sort of courtyard in the middle of the block where it had stood. But there's nothing there now. It was completely consumed. You know, in the kind of way stone buildings usually don't end up." Then he chuckled to himself. "Sorry. The locals are baffled, since apparently no one knew there was a building back there."

"I brought down the protective spells," I said. I had left that bit out of my tale as well.

"You did *what?*" Audrey demanded, nearly dropping her teacup in shock.

But before I could answer, there was another sound at the door to the Square. This time it was the sound of it opening. I looked up to see Barnardo stepping inside, Miss Snooty Cat in his arms. I grabbed my phone out of my pocket and looked at the screen.

A quarter after eight. In other words, sunset.

The time for Houdini's decision had come.

ELEVEN

I could feel Houdini trembling in my lap, but he wasn't speaking to me. He only stood up straighter, locking eyes with Miss Snooty Cat, who gave him the slowest, most disdainful cat wink back at him. Then she moved ever so slightly, just enough to let Barnardo know that she wanted to be put down.

The minute her paws were on the ground, she headed back outside to hop up on one of a pair of white cast-iron chairs that sat beside a similar white cast-iron table on the patio. Then she lifted a single paw, gave it an irritated flick, then proceeded to groom herself. For all the world as if she wasn't waiting for anything, just enjoying the evening as it turned into night.

"Houdini?" I said.

"Please wait here, Tabitha," he said as he hopped down from my lap. "I won't be long."

Barnardo was still standing in the doorway, as if holding the door for the dog, who brushed past him. Only then did he come inside and stroll over to the table where Liam, Audrey and I were sitting together.

"Hello, Barnardo," Audrey said. "We don't usually see you at this time of day. Is everything all right?"

"Quite. Just having a stroll," he said.

I studied his face intently, but if he realized that anything of import was happening out on the patio behind him, he gave no sign of it. I watched past him as Houdini hopped up onto the chair opposite of the one Miss Snooty Cat was perched on, then sat with rigid precision. Like he was hoping to impress her with all of his best obedience school discipline, sitting like a champ and never once looking for the expected treat.

"Miss Snooty Cat's idea?" I asked, as I shifted my gaze back to Barnardo.

"No," he said, giving me a funny look. Which, in a normal world, would be the correct look to give someone who had just suggested someone let their cat take them out for walkies. But we didn't live in a normal world.

Did he even know Miss Snooty Cat wasn't really a cat? I honestly couldn't tell. He never seemed to talk to her the way I did with Houdini. Which I had done even before I realized he was capable of talking back to me just as fluently.

So, did Barnardo just silently do her bidding?

"Do you see my dog and your cat out there?" I asked, inwardly flinching at calling Houdini a dog. But that's what Barnardo thought he was.

"I might've had an ulterior motive for coming out at this hour," Barnardo said, as if he hadn't heard my question at all.

"What's that?" Audrey asked.

Barnardo nimbly slid into the open chair between Audrey and me and leaned forward, the classic posture of Barnardo Daley when he has secrets to dish.

"There was a murder in Geneva," he said with relish.

"A murder," I said, trading glances first with Audrey and then with Liam. Liam, who had just put his phone away, whipped it back out to start scrolling the news feeds again.

"I know, I know, it's not likely to involve us at all," Barnardo said with a wistful sigh. "It's half a world away. It's just, murder in our community is so rare. And I've rather gotten the sleuthing bug. But I guess I'll just have to follow the details on this one from afar."

I bit back an unkind response about his level of involvement in our last two cases. I mean, he had been helpful in all the ways he could be. I wasn't questioning that.

But when I had faced down both of the murderers, the second time entirely on my own, he had also been what I would call "afar."

"Well, ask not for whom the bell tolls, right?" Audrey said. "There aren't enough of us in the magical community not to mourn all our losses, no matter how remote they might seem."

Liam glanced up at her, the hungry gleam for more knowledge in his eyes, but he could see this was not the moment to ask about population counts and life expectancy.

But I did see him open up his note taking app, and then his thumbs were flying, taking down all the questions he was sure to ask the both of us later.

"Of course, of course," Barnardo said. But I actually respected him more for not really trying to sound contrite about it. I, too, had been bitten by the sleuthing bug.

Of course, in this case I couldn't exactly call myself remote from the victim.

"Who died?" I burst out, as casually as I could. Which wasn't terribly casually; I had all but shouted that question.

"I don't recall the first name, but he was part of the Talbot family. Have you heard of them?" Barnardo asked, looking from me to Audrey. We both shook our heads, but he wasn't disappointed. Now he had the opportunity to spill the beans himself.

"They owned a certain bookshop, hidden in the back ways of Geneva," he said, leaning forward over the table again as if afraid someone might overhear us. "The Talbot Repository. It's quite famous, or perhaps I should say *infamous*."

"Infamous for what?" I asked. I reached for my teacup to take a casual little sip, but found it empty.

"It operated in a sort of gray area," Barnardo said. "That was why it wasn't part of the Geneva magical community proper."

"Actually, that community itself is largely broken up into discreet units," Liam said, to all of our surprise. "Sorry. Steph has been giving me a few things to read. Not about magic itself, but about history and geography and like that."

"He's not wrong," Audrey said. "I've never been there, but my mother had a semester abroad there during her academy days. There are a few places that have two or three buildings together inside the protective wards, but nothing like the Square, let alone the entire neighborhoods like in Paris or London."

"Manhattan has a lot of isolated magical buildings," I said.

"But they're all connected by the magical subway," Liam said.

"That's true," I said.

"Well, all I'm saying is, the Talbot Book Repository was even more isolated than other buildings in Geneva," Barnardo said, pulling everyone's attention back to his own story. "And deliberately so. The elder Talbots did not get on well with the High Council. At all."

"Was their death considered suspicious?" I asked.

Barnardo blinked at me, and I realized he hadn't yet told us that the parents were dead, or that they had died together. But he quickly recovered. "No, just a prosaic tragedy. Which, I guess, is pretty ironic, given how many powerful wizards would've loved the opportunity to take them out."

"Take them out?" Audrey gasped. "What kind of people were they?"

"Blackmailers," Barnardo said. I expected him to start cackling any minute now. He was already rubbing his hands together in delight. But he pulled himself back from the emotional edge to add in a calmer voice, "Or so the rumor has it."

"There's nothing in the prosaic news feeds about a body," Liam said, setting his phone facedown on the table.

"No, there wouldn't be," Barnardo said. "The magical authorities scrubbed the site before the prosaic first responders could get a proper look at anything."

"That's where all the stone went, then," Liam guessed, but Barnardo just shrugged. Architecture was not an interest of his.

"So Prospero's body is in the custody of the Geneva authorities, then," I said.

"That's his name! Prospero!" Barnardo said with relief. But then he gave me a suspicious look. "How do you know him?"

"Bookshop networking," I said, and bit my lip. That was a total lie, and I could see Barnardo probing it in his mind. Would my uncles be part of an association that also included the alleged blackmailing gray-area Talbot Book Repository?

Apparently the answer was yes, as he just shrugged, but in response to my original statement. "I assume they have the body that was found there. I don't know if they've even had a chance to identify it yet. The Talbots had two sons, both adults. Or it could've been some other employee all together."

"Are the authorities investigating the blackmail angle?" Liam asked.

Barnardo shrugged again, this time with a little laugh. "I'm sorry. I got a little too excited over what was really a very small piece of news. It's all happened only in the last hour, and what has passed through the whisper network is sparse enough. But I admit I was tickled by our local angle."

"Tickled?" Liam repeated with barely contained distaste.

But Audrey asked the important question. "Our local angle?"

"Oh, yes," Barnardo said, and that gleam was back in his eye. "Rumor has it, one of the wizards that the Talbots had blackmail material on was our own local wizard. You know, *the* Wizard."

"Oh, I'm skeptical about that," Audrey said.

"What part?" Barnardo asked.

"All of it," she said, and shot me a look.

But what could I say? I didn't know the Wizard at all, and even after meeting him—whenever that actually happened—I doubt I'd come away with enough knowledge to have any clue what he may or may not have done that would be blackmailable.

"Well, it's all still breaking news," Barnardo said as he got up from the table. I looked behind him and saw no sign of Houdini. Just Miss Snooty Cat, sitting alone at the café table, looking at a point at the back of Barnardo's head. For all the world like she was giving him telepathic commands.

"It's probably better if we don't speculate about the pasts of people we know nothing about, then," Audrey said.

"Of course. I didn't mean any harm. And obviously it's not just the Wizard, anyway. I've heard a few other names bandied about. Prominent names. Of course, I'll want to verify the details before we start thinking of anyone as a suspect," Barnardo said. Then he glanced at the clock on the teashop wall. "It's getting late. I should get Miss Snooty Cat back inside. Did you know there have been coyotes spotted roaming the streets in the suburbs?"

"I'm sure we're all perfectly safe inside the Square," I told him. Although I was more acutely aware of how much I didn't like not seeing where Houdini was at that moment. And if he was still okay.

"I'll be sure to check in with all my usual sources before breakfast tomorrow," Barnardo said. "It'll be nighttime here, but daytime in Geneva between now and then. I'm sure they'll know a lot more by the time we're sitting down to tea and scones."

My stomach chose that moment to growl loudly. But Barnardo was already gone, out the door and with Miss Snooty Cat already in his arms. She looked back over his shoulder at me, her green eyes shining out of the growing shadows like eerie beacons. But as easily seen as those eyes were, I had no idea what emotion lurked behind them. Was she gloating, because she had Houdini in her power? Or was she sulking, because she didn't?

Well, I would know soon enough. I just had to find Houdini.

But as I made my excuses to Audrey and Liam, anxious to both find Houdini and to find something to eat while I waited to hear from Steph, a single thought was stuck in my head, running on a loop.

The safe in the floor of the office of the Talbot Repository had been large. Far larger than needed to contain the book Steph and I had been there to pick up.

And that safe had also been completely empty.

At the time, I had assumed the bookshop had been robbed of a cashbox, perhaps a few other rare books besides the esoteric one we had been after.

But what if that hadn't been the target at all? What if the book we wanted was only collateral damage?

What if someone had been after the blackmail material? And now that they had gotten it, what were they about to do next?

And what if the Wizard really was implicated in something? Or worse, had done something?

Okay, that was more than a single thought. But I wasn't lying about the running on a loop thing. Those questions just kept going round and round. And there was nothing I could do at the moment to bring myself any closer to any of the answers.

Not without Steph.

TWELVE

I found Houdini curled up on the window seat of my nook on the fourth floor of the bookshop. It was a cozy place when warmed by the light through the south-facing window. We spent many long hours there together, cuddling and reading books.

But in the darkness, alone, with no book in sight, he just looked so sad. He was curled up, but not in a napping kind of a way. Rather, it was a very tense folding in on himself, his nose tucked under his back knee but his eyes wide open.

"Houdini?" I said as I came closer to sit beside him. He said nothing, but moved at once to crawl into my lap. "Are you all right?" I asked.

"I am well enough," he said.

"How did your meeting with Miss Snooty Cat go?" I asked.

"Please don't be angry, but I agreed to her offer," he said.

"You don't seem happy about it," I said as neutrally as I could.

"I went out to that table on the patio so sure I had thought through every angle," he said, and his little rat terrier-chihuahua form on my lap went into full tremble mode. "I was so sure I knew what I was getting into. After talking with Steph, I had come up with the exact terms I was willing to agree to. What I wanted from her, what I was willing to do in return, I had it all spelled out."

"Maybe we should have written it up like a proper contract," I said. "I'm sorry I wasn't here to help you with that."

"She wouldn't have agreed to it anyway," Houdini said. "I asked. Nothing in writing. Our words spoken aloud are iron-clad enough."

"Did she cast a magical binding on your agreement or something?" I asked.

"I don't think so?" he said. "My honor binds me. Or so she said. But it feels true. I'm not sure, but I think she knows I'm a dragon. Or she suspects. Anyway, it felt loaded, when she used the word honor."

"So what happened?" I asked.

And the trembling kicked up another notch. I held him close, and he nosed under my hand until I took the hint and started petting him.

"I gave her my terms. I was very clear. I felt completely confident in what we were agreeing to, up until the moment we sealed the deal with our vows," he said. "But afterwards, there was just something in her eyes, something in the way she was looking down at me. I think I messed up somewhere, but I don't know where. And the more I try to remember what was said, the less I'm sure that I was as clear as I thought. I think her answers sounded like the right ones at the time, but when I think back now, I don't think she was saying exactly what I thought she was saying."

"She negotiated like the slipperiest of lawyers?" I guessed.

"Yes, just that," he agreed. "And now I don't know what's going to happen."

"What did she say would happen first?" I asked. "I mean, is she even going to help you?"

"Oh, yes. She promised to have answers for me in a couple of days. That much I believe."

"It's what you offered in return that's worrying you," I said with a sigh. "Oh, Houdini. I'm not sure if I would've been any help to you if I'd been out there with you. Miss Snooty Cat sounds very crafty, and she likely would've conned us both. But I still wish I'd been there."

"I wish you'd been there too," he said, then craned his head up to lick the tip of my nose. Not my favorite of his doggy gestures, but I let it go. Then he looked me directly in the eyes, his own brown eyes so strangely intelligent inside his little dog head. "Can we call for Steph, please?"

"You don't need my permission for that," I said. "I'm waiting to talk to him about some things myself. But he might be busy."

"I just called him," Houdini said after the briefest of pauses. "He said he'll be along momentarily."

"Do you want to tell me about this boon you promised Miss Snooty Cat, or do you want to wait until Steph is here?" I asked.

"She still hasn't told me what she wants from me," he said. "I'm just afraid that she managed to side-step all the limitations I tried to put on to what I was offering. Her answers were so twisty. I thought they meant one thing, but now I can see how they may all have meant another."

"Matagots are a lot like sphinxes in that way," Steph said, suddenly there with us in the semidarkness of the nook. He waved a hand in the air and the bookshop obliged to bring the lights up to their more comfortable level. Then he came over to sit beside us on the window seat. "There's a reason she would only deal with you alone, Houdini. Her powers of obfuscation work best when she's only using them on one mind at a time. If either Tabitha or I had been with you, you wouldn't have even needed us to do a thing for your own mind to have been clearer. Our mere presence would've diluted her power."

"If I had known that, I definitely wouldn't have let you go out there alone," I said.

"Steph had warned me," Houdini told me. "I thought I was prepared. I didn't feel like she was doing anything to cloud my mind until afterwards."

"Matagots are dangerous things when they choose to be," Steph said. "But they can also be sources of great fortune for others if that's what they choose."

"Barnardo certainly seems fond of her, which I don't think would be true if she were actually evil," I forced myself to admit. "I just wish she hadn't chosen to be malevolent to Houdini."

"Oh, I don't know if that's necessarily the case," Steph said. "Did she offer to help?" he asked Houdini.

"She did," he said grudgingly. "But she negotiated around my limitations on my boon."

"Well, I did warn you she likely would," Steph said with a sympathetic wince. "But, again, it doesn't necessarily mean she wishes you any harm. Obfuscating your mind and negotiating only on her terms is just her nature. You won't really know what she wants of you until she asks it. But, Houdini, if it's something truly out of bounds, just call for me. She is a creature of magic, but she doesn't have a wizard's mind for bindings. She can't hold you in any way that the Wizard and I can't find a way to break if you need us to."

"I see. Thank you," Houdini said.

"Don't mention it. Hopefully, it won't even come up. She's working on her end of things now, right?"

"She said she was," Houdini said.

"Then I'm sure she is. Let's just wait to hear what she has and what she wants in return," Steph said. "If my guess is right, she'll choose the boon based on the value of what she finds for you. If she can't find much, she won't ask you for much."

"Well, that's something, I guess," I said.

But Houdini blinked at me in amazement. "How is that comforting? Now I have to decide whether I hope she doesn't find much so she won't demand much, or hoping she finds a lot even though it will cost me a lot. And I don't even know how long I'll be waiting!"

"I'm sorry," I said.

"I'm going to take a walk and have a think," Houdini said, and jumped off my lap.

I wanted to say something, like to tell him to be safe or not go far or... something. But Steph put a hand on my knee and gave me a silent shake of his head. So I said nothing. I just watched Houdini disappear down the long aisle between rows of bookshelves, heading for the staircase at the heart of the shop.

"I'm sorry if we pulled you away from anything important," I said to Steph. "Have you spoken with the Wizard? Not that I'm pressuring you or anything!" I rushed to add, and could feel my cheeks flushing hotly. "You said it would happen soon, me meeting him, and I totally believe you! It's just, I've heard some things about that bookshop the Talbots own. And about the Wizard."

The soft smile he had been giving me at my admittedly dorky rush of words faded by the time I was done speaking.

"What have you heard about the Wizard and the Talbots?" he asked with a worried frown.

"Just rumors from Barnardo, and vague ones at that," I said.

"Tell me."

"I guess the Talbots—I mean the Talbot parents who died two weeks ago—were blackmailers. And they might have had dirt on the Wizard as well as other prominent wizards," I said. "I don't know what any of it might have been. But I was worried it might have been in the safe. I mean, there were probably things in there that someone stole when they stabbed Prospero, potentially dangerous things. More than just the book we were looking for."

"I was not aware of this," Steph said, and his frown deepened.

"I'm sure whatever it is, about the Wizard, it can't possibly be true," I said.

He gave me a steady look that I couldn't read at all. But inside, I was feeling like I was being pretty stupid. How could I be so sure something wasn't true, when I didn't even know what the something *was*? And who was I to judge the moral character of the Wizard, whom I had never even met?

But that look was worrying me. "Steph?" I said when I couldn't bear it any longer.

"The Wizard is old. Not as old as Agatha, but nearly so," he said at last. "I don't know any of the details, and I've never pried, but he does occasionally mention things. Things he did when he was younger, centuries ago. Things he regrets now."

"Bad things?" I asked and realized I was whispering, even though we were completely alone inside the bookshop. "I mean, people can regret things they did that weren't illegal or immoral, just ill-advised. Or maybe unkind."

"I don't know," Steph said. "But I'll have to at least tell him about these rumors. He should know about that. Not that he gives even the smallest of thoughts about his reputation. It might take a bit of work for me to get him to see it might be a problem that needs to be addressed." Then he sighed, as if the conversation he hadn't even started having yet was already exhausting him.

"But he knows about the fire and the missing book?" I asked.

"He does."

"And me?" I asked, whispering again. And I wasn't even saying out loud the thing I did.

But Steph knew what I meant, anyway. "That is what he's looking into right now."

"What do you mean, looking into?" I asked, fighting down a wave of panic.

"He's in Geneva," Steph said, as if that were the most normal thing in the world for his notoriously reclusive boss to be doing. Traveling across the world to... what?

"What's he doing in Geneva? Like, specifically?" I asked.

"Nothing that should be alarming you like this," he said, and framed my face with his hands before giving me a light kiss.

A strangely calming kiss. But it couldn't possibly have magic in it, as much as it felt like it did. The silver amulet on my wrist would ask permission now before lowering my naturally very high magical protections to let such an influence in.

It was just him.

Or a different kind of magic, anyway.

"He was summoned to Geneva by the High Council," Steph told me as he sat back. But he was still closer to me than he had been the moment before. And his hands were clasping mine as they rested on my lap. "I had already told him what happened when we were there, and he had been intending to go, anyway. But this way, responding to a summons, he didn't have to risk explaining himself."

"Why was he summoned?" I asked.

"They are trying to figure out what happened to the protective magical barrier that you took down," he said. "The Wizard wanted to see the broken magic for himself before speaking with you. What you did... Well, I don't need to tell you it was no small thing. No one is going to even consider it was the work of a single person. That might be enough to keep you free from suspicion."

"I guess it's ironic, then," I said with a dry laugh.

"What's that?" he asked.

"Every time something like this happens, something that seems like it means I'm more powerful than I ever could've dreamed of, I always end up feeling less safe than I did before. Shouldn't having power make me feel... well, powerful?"

Steph didn't answer for the longest time. We both just looked down at our fingers twined together in my lap. But then he looked up at my face, his brown eyes darker than ever. "I wished I could tell you something heartening at this moment. Something affirming or whatever."

"But?" I said. I didn't want to know what came next. But I had to know.

"But I'm afraid that you're right to be afraid," he said. "I'm afraid that the more power you find in yourself, the more danger that you're in."

"In a way, that is affirming," I said, my tone far more jaunty than my actual feelings. But I could see how much this conversation was disturbing him. He was feeling just as overwhelmed as I was, in his own way.

"What do you mean?" he asked, raising an eyebrow at me.

"Well, it's nice to know when I'm right," I said with a shrug. That got the tiniest of laughs out of him.

Which was great.

But the last thing I ever wanted to be right about was that the correct response to the situation I was in was to be afraid.

CHAPTER

THIRTEEN

Steph and I stayed in that window seat together until just before midnight, when the Wizard returned to the Tower and summoned him away. With one last kiss and a promise to see me as soon as he could, he was gone.

Again.

I found Houdini already curled up at the foot of the bed, although as soon as I slipped into bed myself, he sleepily crept up to the top of the bed so I could let him under the covers. He tucked up behind my knees, and we both slept surprisingly soundly, given how much was weighing on both of us.

I was still feeling unusually mellow in the morning as I showered and dressed. Shouldn't I be on tenterhooks, not knowing what was going on? Maybe. But I just wasn't.

And neither was Houdini. He just yawned widely as he watched me pull on my sneakers, and then the two of us headed down the stairs together.

It might've been comical from an outside perspective, the way both of us shrieked and jumped into the air to find people in my uncles' kitchen, apparently waiting for us to come down the stairs. I even felt my power bristling, lifting up my hair, and then the soft touch of the amulet at the back of my mind, asking if I wanted it to let go of its control of my power so I could use all of it to smite...

Audrey and Liam. It was Audrey and Liam.

Standing in my uncles' kitchen.

I just stood there in the doorway, blinking at them, as my power fizzled and faded away. Which was still a new feeling, and would've been kind of nice if I wasn't so distracted.

"Oh, no. Who's dead?" I asked, and flailed numb hands until I managed to grasp and cling to the doorway.

"No one's dead," Liam said, confused.

"We didn't mean to startle you," Audrey said. "We just had some information for you on your case, and in light of what it was, I decided not to open the teashop today."

"You're not opening the teashop?" I asked. This felt even more like a someone just died scenario.

"*She's* not opening the teashop," Liam said. "I am. She's going out with you today."

"If you want!" Audrey rushed to add.

"Maybe we better back up," I said.

"Yeah, I think we should," Liam said, and reached out slowly as if afraid I might lash out at him like a nervous animal. But when I didn't snap at him or set him on fire, he took my arm and guided me over to the dining booth built into the wall of the tiny kitchen space.

"We brought tea and scones," Audrey said, gesturing to the cups, saucers and plates she had already arranged over the tabletop. Then she picked up a few of the pumpkin peanut butter treats she baked for dogs and looked around. "Did Houdini run clear back up the stairs?"

"I'm here," he said, emerging from under the sofa in my uncles' living room. "You startled us."

"I'm sorry. Somehow I thought it would be a *nice* surprise," Audrey said.

I lifted the lid on the teapot and inhaled the unmistakable bergamot scent of Audrey's special tea blend. Audrey's special highly caffeinated tea blend. I poured some into my cup, added an unhealthy amount of sugar, and drank it down before finally saying, "Okay. I'm ready. Start from the top."

"I think I know who killed Prospero Talbot and burned the bookshop to the ground," Liam said.

"His brother," I guessed as I made myself a second cup of syrupy sweet, strong tea.

"Yeah. Antonio Talbot," Liam said, flipping through pages in his notebook. I knew he started a fresh notebook every time we started a new case. He hadn't had one on him the day before. But in the time between, he had filled an entire Moleskin with his tiny writing.

"But he was the chief suspect anyway, right?" I said.

"Yes, but there are going to be complications with the magical authorities bringing him in," Liam said. "He's not been living in magical communities since he finished his schooling twelve years ago."

"What, wait?" I said. The tea, caffeinated as it was, was still taking entirely too long to hit my brain that morning.

"He's been living in my world. The prosaic world," Liam said. "But there's more to it than that."

"That would explain why he didn't inherit his parents' shop, though, wouldn't it?" Audrey put in. "If he left the magical community completely to live a prosaic life, I don't think by law he could inherit anything, even if his parents left it to him."

"He would have to choose," I said. I had taken a few basic magical law classes, back when being a lawyer had felt like something a non-magic-user could do.

It wasn't. No one could master all that they needed to know without using a ton of magic. The laws that govern our communities are beyond complex.

But before admitting it wasn't for me, I had learned a couple of things. "If he had been named in the will, the executor of the estate would have to track him down and inform him. Then he'd have to choose, come back to our world and remain there if he wanted the property. Or turn it down and remain in the prosaic world as he was."

"Do we know if that was done?" Liam asked, looking at me over the top of the open notebook in his hands.

"I don't think so?" I said. "From what his brother said, I gather it was only left to Prospero. If he was the only named heir in the will, there would have been no need to find Antonio at all."

"But he must have heard about it somehow," Audrey said. "Even living in the prosaic world, he must've heard that his parents were dead."

"Maybe his brother told him?" I said. "Or maybe he found out some other way. I guess that theory makes more sense. I got the sense that Antonio had only recently shown up angry about not inheriting his fair share. And I don't think that would've happened if he'd known about his parents since they died."

"So he still has contacts in the magic world," Audrey said. "Interesting."

"I'm missing something," I guessed, looking from her to Liam.

"Well, he's not exactly anonymous in the prosaic world," Liam said.

"You mean he's famous?" I asked.

"No, nothing like that," Audrey said.

"He has a rap sheet," Liam said. "He's been in and out of institutions pretty much since he left home for the prosaic world twelve years ago."

"You mean prison?" I asked.

"Prison, but also mental health facilities," Liam said.

"It's possible that's why he left home in the first place," Audrey said. "Our community isn't exactly great with dealing with mental health issues. He might've thought he'd get better care out there."

"Did he?" I asked, but then quickly added, "Never mind. You said he'd been in and out of institutions. That doesn't sound like success."

"Actually, from what I've gotten a hold of from his medical files..." Liam said, rapidly turning pages in his notebook even as his ears turned bright red. I had a pretty good idea that he wasn't supposed to have access to those files. But Liam always found a way. "Yes, here's the timeline. He was still under the care of a doctor and a therapist, but was living on his own. He has a job—I suppose it's not ironic that it's in a bookstore—and a loft apartment in Geneva."

"A bookstore? But in the prosaic world, right?" I said.

"Yes. He's just a low-level clerk, and it's one of the big chains. Nothing so grand as a repository of banned books in a Gothic church or anything," Liam said.

"Have the prosaic authorities picked him up?" I asked.

"There's no reason for them to," he said. "They don't know there was a murder, and investigating an arson in a building that wasn't even supposed to be there isn't exactly a top priority."

"There might be lingering effects of the barrier, too," I mused. "They might not look into it because looking into it would put the magical community in danger."

"I thought you blew that thing apart?" Audrey said.

"I don't know *what* I did," I admitted.

And immediately thought of Steph. Whom I hadn't heard from yet. Whatever the Wizard had learned from examining the remains of my handiwork in Geneva, it was still a mystery to me.

"Our authorities could go out into the prosaic world and retrieve him," I said. "If they were sure he was the murderer, they would act on that."

"As much as I am information guy in the prosaic world, I don't have any way of knowing what's going on in your world," Liam said with a wistful sigh.

"It's a shame we don't have magical computers you can hack," Audrey said, giving him a teasing grin.

I wasn't sure that was entirely true. The sheriff and deputy who were in charge of the part of Minneapolis that included the Square had tablets they used constantly. And I was pretty sure they weren't just off-the-shelf prosaic tablets.

Although I was unlikely to get a hold of one to take a closer look anytime soon. So I let Audrey's point stand.

And tried to ignore the way the two of them were making goo-goo eyes at each other.

"So why are you taking the day off from the teashop again?" I asked. Not that either of them had told me anything about that yet.

"Oh, that was the last bit Liam wanted to tell you," Audrey said, making encouraging gestures at Liam and his notebook.

But he just closed it and set it down on the tabletop in front of him, folding his hands over it before leaning forward to say, "There's someone right here in the Square that the two of you really need to talk to."

"Barnardo?" I guessed. He probably had a lot more details on those blackmailing rumors than he had had the morning before.

But Liam was shaking his head.

"It's Violenta Court," Audrey said, unable to let Liam build up the suspense any longer.

"Violenta Court? The fashion boutique owner?" I said, confused.

Granted, I had been meaning for months now to stop in there and acquire some new clothes. After years of having mandated academy uniforms be the bulk of my wardrobe, what I'd been getting by on since coming to the Square was a small number of items that were starting to really show both their age and the frequency with which they went through the laundry.

But this wasn't about a shopping trip. And while I knew Violenta Court well enough to exchange nods of hello and the occasional good morning, what she had to do with anything happening in Switzerland was more than I could guess.

"She went to school with the Talbot brothers," Audrey told me. "Prospero was a year ahead of her, and Antonio was a year behind. But she knew them both."

"Are you sure?" I asked. "I've been to some academies where

knowing all the students in your own year was all but impossible. Unless it was a really small school..."

But Liam was lifting the front cover of his notebook, pulling out a carefully clipped square of paper. He put it on the table in front of me. It was a photograph.

I recognized a younger Violenta Court at once. The pink hair that turned to rose at the tips was hard to miss. And the young man next to her, if I added a decade and a half of years and an intense amount of recent stress, could be Prospero.

Which would make the other young man in the picture Antonio. The one staring into the camera, his eyes just barely visible through his thick, unruly bangs of dark hair. The one standing with his arms crossed and his chest puffed up in a cocky pose. He was more attractive than I was expecting, albeit with a strong bad boy energy that I had always personally found unappealing.

But I knew I was a minority opinion in that. And from the way Violenta was leaning ever so slightly his way, as if drawn towards him by a magnetic pull, I was pretty sure she wouldn't have agreed with me then.

Although whether she would agree with me now remained to be seen.

"We should go talk to Violenta," I said.

Steph could find me anywhere when he finally needed me, when my wait to hear from him would finally end.

And at least this way, I was doing something productive with my time. Not that doing my actual job was *unproductive*, of course.

But I really wanted to hear what Violenta remembered from her academy days.

FOURTEEN

At first, I thought the three of us were going down to the teashop first so that Audrey could give Liam some last-minute instructions on running the business while she was out. But the minute we stepped inside, Liam went straight to the back to start filling up the pastry case with scones and rolls left in the warmers after Audrey's early morning baking session. Audrey went behind the counter to start the kettle. Then she took down an unlabeled tea tin and scooped some of the contents into an empty steeping bag.

"What are we doing?" I asked conversationally.

"Oh, this is Violenta's special blend," Audrey said. "It's a white tea with floral elements."

"A blend just for her? And you keep a whole tin of it?" I asked. I tried not to feel left out. I mean, *I* didn't have a special tea. But then, I liked variety. And I loved drinking whatever Audrey was most excited about at any given moment.

"She's a loyal customer," Audrey said. "One of my first, actually. She had stopped coming to Loose Leaves when Agatha lost her tea mojo, but she was willing to give me a try on my very first day. Luckily, I could put together what she wanted perfectly on the first try."

"Well, that's hardly surprising. You're amazing," I said. The tea kettle beeped and shut off without quite coming to a boil, and Audrey poured the water over the tea-bag in one of her take-away cups. Liam was just emerging from the back room with a tray full of pastries, and she snatched two of the scones in passing, wrapping them in waxed paper, then dropping them into a white paper bag.

"All right. I think we're all ready," Audrey said, licking a bit of sugar off her finger that had crumbled away from what I guessed by the scent had been a lemon and rosemary scone. She slipped out from behind the counter after giving Liam a quick peck on the cheek. Liam, of course, flushed a bright red. But he also held the tray out for me surreptitiously.

I snatched one of the lemon and rosemary scones, then hustled to follow Audrey out the door and onto the Square.

"It's earlier in the day than her usual teatime," Audrey said as we cut across the orchard, skirting around the hedge maze to the far side of the Square. "She comes in every day at two o'clock precisely. But provided she doesn't have any customers there right as she opens, I think the tea and scones will persuade her to talk to us."

"I don't know if she'll be able to tell us anything really useful," I said. "I doubt she knows anything that is going to help me find that book. Unless she knows where the brother is hiding. If he even has it."

"We won't come out of it knowing anything less," Audrey pointed out.

"True," I said. "Plus, I've been meaning to see inside her shop since I got here. I just never seem to find the time."

"Same," Audrey said.

We arrived at the shop to find the door unlocked. A little bell over the door announced our arrival with a silvery chime that echoed around the shop interior, a touch of magic added to boost its prosaic use.

The shop interior was about the same size as the Loose Leaves Teashop, but every inch of that space was stuffed with racks of clothing. And yet the total effect wasn't cluttered or crowded at all. The racks were magically suspended in three-tiered arrangements that floated nearer or farther, responding to subtle cues I didn't even know I was giving. But somehow the shop or the racks or *something* knew the minute my eye was caught by anything, and that item would be floated forward while other items faded back.

I looked down at my button-up shirt and capris. The knees on my capris were very shiny, the material so thin it was a miracle it hadn't worn through already. And the original vivid pink of my top had faded to something that could only generously be described as salmon color.

"Look," I said, distracting Audrey from her scan of the store for any sign of Violenta. "This skirt has pockets."

"Everything here has pockets. Witches *need* pockets," a woman said from behind us. She had a rich voice that filled the space around us without feeling overly loud. The sort of voice a good stage actor would have. Which probably wasn't a coincidence. Her level of projection sounded trained to my ear.

I turned to see the familiar figure of Violenta Court just emerging from a door in the back that was immediately covered again by racks of clothes, like she had a secret entrance to her office or something. I immediately felt tiny in her presence, as I always did. She topped out at six feet and was as wide across the shoulders as any Scotsman competing in the caber toss. Despite that linebacker build, her look was all feminine, with gauzy layers and flowing skirts and lots of tinkling jewelry.

But mostly it was her hair, piled high in a do that went beyond beehive into Marie Antoinette territory. And it went from a cotton candy pink close to her scalp to a rich rose color at the ends, making the whole updo look like a delicious confectionary.

"Violenta!" Audrey said. She thrust out the cup and bag of pastries. "I brought you a bribe."

"A bribe?" Violenta said, but with a wide, dazzling smile. "I'm open to bribes. What are you looking for in return? A discount, perhaps?"

"Just a little conversation," Audrey said as Violenta peeled the lid off her tea, then put her face close to breathe in the floral-scented steam. She closed her eyes as she soaked it in, then opened them again to smile at Audrey once more.

"Anything for you, darling. It's a little crowded for three in my office, but I can tell a few of these racks to give us a little space around the counter if you don't mind standing?"

"Not at all," Audrey said with a glance at me.

"Sounds perfect," I said.

Violenta took a sip from her tea, but her eyes were on me the whole time. Then she strolled over to the counter—the racks indeed parting before her to give her plenty of room—and set down her tea before turning to look me over more thoroughly.

I felt just how shabby my clothing was at that moment. And I was really regretting not making the time to stop in before.

But Violenta just said, "We've not really met yet, but I know who you are, Tabitha Greene. But I can't imagine what you'd want to talk to me about." Then her eyes flitted over to Audrey. "Sorry, Audrey, darling. I appreciate the bribe, but I know which of you this is really about, don't I?"

"We both wanted to talk to you," Audrey said.

"But she's the one who's going to be asking all the questions," Violenta said.

"Not *all* the questions," I said.

"It's all right. I'm just curious what I can help you with, is all," she said. She took another sip of tea, then leaned forward with her elbows on the counter. "Fire away."

I looked over at Audrey, who took the clipped photograph out of her pocket and set it on the counter in front of Violenta. Violenta glanced at it, but I could tell the instant when it clicked in her mind what she was looking at. Then she scooped it up and brought it closer to her face, tilting it to catch better light.

"Oh, my," she said. "This was a lifetime ago." Then she looked up at me. "I know what's happened. I suppose everyone does. But I don't know how it involves you."

"I was shopping for a book," I said simply. Not remotely the whole truth, but it was, at least, wholly true.

"They would be able to help you with that, sure enough," she said, looking down at the photograph again. "Only I hate to point it out, but you already work in one of the world's largest bookshops."

"It was a special kind of book," I said.

Violenta bit at her lip, but in the end just nodded as she set the picture back down. "Yes, they would be able to help you with that, too."

"You knew them well?" Audrey asked.

"Knew them well?" Violenta repeated, as if tasting the words the way a sommelier would taste a wine, to find its elements and qualities. "I would say I knew them quite well, intensely well, for a few years. But it's been years since then, and I don't know I would say the same about either of them now."

"So you were close friends at the academy but fell out of touch after?" I asked.

"Not immediately after," she said with a wistful sigh.

"Were you dating either of them?" I ventured. Because I was getting vibes of an intense romance, then a rending breakup, and parts of my brain were cooking up possible love triangle theories.

But Violenta just laughed. "Oh, no. I've never been into boys, darling."

"Oh. Sorry," I said, but she waved my apology away.

At least I hadn't voiced my suspicions of her literally leaning towards bad boys out loud. I was embarrassed enough just for having thought it.

"No, I was close friends with both of them. We were in a club of sorts. Nothing officially recognized by the academy or anything. More just a group of kids with common backgrounds. Other kids were part of it more casually, but the three of us were really the core of the group."

"What drew you together?" I asked.

"Bad parents," Violenta said. "We were all very driven to get away from our family homes as soon as possible. We planned together ways to make sure we didn't have to go home on breaks. Pretending to visit each other while secretly spending the winter holiday in Paris, for instance. But we really focused on what we would do after graduation."

I chewed at my lip. That would explain Antonio's fleeing to the prosaic world, if he wanted to escape his parents. But it didn't remotely explain Prospero not only choosing to stay, but choosing to continue working with his parents every day of his life.

I was still trying to work out what to say when Audrey asked, "How did that work out for you? Did you get away?"

"I did," Violenta said, but guardedly. "I opened this shop just before my twentieth birthday. But that first year out of the academy was... very rough."

"You didn't stay in school for higher studies?" Audrey asked.

"No, I knew that wasn't for me," she said, and summoned that same bright smile again. It looked genuine. "But the Talbot brothers both did."

"What did they study?" I asked.

"They both have degrees in bibliomancy and library studies," Violenta said.

"Like they were looking to go into the family business?" I asked, and she nodded. "But I thought they were in your group because they wanted to get away from their parents?"

"It's complicated, isn't it?" she said and took a long sip of tea before going on. "My case was always more straightforward than theirs. I was never conflicted about my decision to cut my family out of my life, and I did it just as soon as I could. But theirs was... well, just more complicated."

"I've heard that their parents were blackmailers," I said.

"I've heard that too," she said. "I've never met them. And the boys... I mean, the Talbot brothers were always vague about what their parents did. But it was always clear to me they were vague because what their parents were up to was illegal, maybe even dangerous."

"So why study bibliomancy, then?" I asked.

Violenta took a deep breath, closing her eyes as she struggled to come to a decision. But when she opened them again, she was just as blithe as before, taking one of the scones out of the bag to crumble off a corner before finally looking back at me. "I guess I can tell you this since I know they never actually did it. But the two of them didn't talk so much about fleeing their parents as killing them and taking over their business."

"Their parents *did* just die," Audrey said.

"I know. I read about it in the papers. Very carefully," Violenta said with cold emphasis. "You know, reading between the lines. I was worried about what it meant. I mean, why now? After all this time? But I still worried. Only from everything that was reported, there is no question it was an accident."

"And, like you said, so much time had passed," I said.

"Exactly," she agreed, and put another piece of scone in her mouth.

"What do you think happened to Prospero?" I asked.

Violenta chewed slowly, then took another sip of tea. Clearly, she was not a woman I could rush to give me answers. But finally she said, "I'm not sure. If you mean what happened the other night in his bookshop, I suppose someone he was dealing with decided to stab their way to a better deal. Because I *know* he's been helping his parents run their side business in forbidden goods for some time, and that would involve a lot of shady people."

"What else would I mean?" I asked.

"Well, if you mean what happened to Prospero after he gradu-ated from the academy, that I really can't tell you," she said. "I managed to stay in better contact with Antonio than Prospero, but that's not saying much. Years have gone by without me hearing from him. But he always sends me some vague postcard, just to let me know he's still alive, if not exactly what you'd call 'okay.' He went into the prosaic world so soon after leaving school he was probably still in the same uniform. I mean, he even had a position waiting for him here in the magical world, but he just chose to walk away from it."

"Not at his parents' bookshop?" I guessed.

"No, it was apprentice to the head librarian at the All-Planes Athenaeum," Violenta said. She turned her attention to the second scone in the bag, giving Audrey and me a chance to exchange a quick look.

That had so nearly been my job. And I would've done anything to get it.

But Antonio Talbot had gotten it, and then just chose to walk away?

"Why?" I found myself asking. At Violenta's raised eyebrow, I clarified, "Why did he walk away from everything?"

"I don't know," she said. "I haven't seen him since I left the acad-emy. That was a year before he went to graduate school, five years before he moved to the prosaic world. I have a few postcards, but there's not much on them that makes any kind of sense. If he was speaking in code, I didn't understand it. And he never left me any way to get back in touch with him. Like I said, I think he just wanted me to know he was still alive."

"Such a strange decision, to just walk away from everything," Audrey said.

But Violenta just shrugged. "I always found Prospero's decision to stay the more puzzling one. But as he wasn't talking to me anymore either, and even more now that he's dead, I guess that will remain a mystery to me."

Then she put the last of the scone in her mouth and regarded the now-empty cup of tea. Like that mystery was already fading from her mind.

Funny, it was having the opposite effect on me. What I wouldn't give for another chance at a conversation with Prospero.

I only hoped it was still possible to have one with Antonio. But I would have to find him first.

CHAPTER

FIFTEEN

It was nearly noon before I finally opened up the bookshop, but that was only a brief foray at the door to turn the sign over before heading up to my nook with way too many bags filled with clothes.

Violenta had refused to let me go without showing me a few things she was sure were perfect for me. I had been skeptical at first. After a lifetime in uniforms, I didn't even know what kind of clothes I wanted to try, let alone what would be perfect for me.

But more than that, as much as her look was perfect for her, it absolutely wouldn't work for me. Even with my silver bracelet keeping my powers under control, I was pretty sure I could set myself on fire just trying to cook with all those gauzy layers floating around me. And they would catch on everything. Best-case scenario: I'd tear all my clothes in the first week wearing them around the bookshop.

Worst-case scenario? Well, my mind tends to go back to setting myself on fire. For good reason. I mean, I've nearly done it so many times.

But that skepticism quickly faded as she summoned this rack or that one, and everything she showed me felt so perfect. Any worry I had that she would try to dress me up like a littler version of her went right out the window when she started showing me pants. They were my preferred length—capris, of course—and looked just a shade dressier than I usually opted for. But they had more pockets than cargo pants.

She even seemed to know what colors I would like best even before I did. Now I had a good start on a new wardrobe, half in black and half in shades of emerald, ruby or sapphire. With a single pink sleeveless blouse, because sometimes even I want to wear just a little pink.

I would have to go back again in a few months to stock up a winter wardrobe, but I was actually kind of looking forward to it.

"There you are," Houdini said accusingly from the window seat when I came in and dumped all my bags on the heavy wooden table that was the heart of my nook.

"Did you need me?" I asked.

"No. Not *specifically*," he said. But there was the tiniest hint of a hurt sniff at the end of that sentence.

"Well, I'm here now," I said, and kissed him on the top of the head. "Did you have any research you wanted me to help you with?"

"No," he said, still a shade sullen, but he was coming around. "I think I'll just wait to hear what Miss Snooty Cat finds before I try looking anymore myself. It's starting to feel a little pointless, you know?"

"I *do* know," I said with feeling. "I guess I'm putting my own research on pause as well. At least until we either find that book, or we definitely don't. Then it's back to square one."

"I hate waiting," Houdini said, and buried his nose behind his curled-in front paws.

"Me, too," I sighed. But it was hard to hide how geeked I still was by my shopping trip. I was just starting to sort my purchases by color so I could start running them through the washing machine in my uncles' laundry room when I felt that unmistakable displacement of air that announced Steph's arrival. I looked up in time to see the wind effect just dropping away from his tousle of dark hair and the folds of the long rainbow-colored robe.

"Steph!" Houdini said, sitting up straighter.

"Greetings, Houdini," Steph said, giving him skritches that carefully avoided his ears. As much as he was disguised as a dog and not a cat, I could swear I heard him purring in pleasure at the touch.

Then Steph turned to kiss me hello, and I had to admit, the sound coming from the back of my throat probably sounded a lot like purring too. But I didn't remotely care.

"Filling your time, I see?" Steph said when he finally stepped back to take in the piles of new clothes on the table.

"I went to talk to Violenta Court about the Talbots. They all knew each other when they were teenagers," I said.

"Really?" Steph said, then took a moment to turn this thought over in his mind.

"I'll admit, what she had to say made things more confused in my mind rather than less," I said. "I went into it pretty sure that Antonio had killed his brother either out of jealousy for the inheritance or possibly because of some sort of mental illness. But now I'm not so sure."

"Family isn't destiny," Steph said, then looked me in the eye when he said, "but the Talbot family has a long, not good history."

"Any word on the book?" I asked hopefully.

"Not yet," he said. But before I could quite start feeling disappointed by that, he said, "I'm here to bring you to meet the Wizard, actually. We've finally finished the necessary preparations for you to come. Both of you, if you'd care to come as well, Houdini."

"I would be honored," Houdini said, sitting up even straighter on the window seat.

"Now?" I said, looking wistfully at the piles of new but not yet washed clothes, and then down at the faded things I was still wearing. I mean, they had felt good enough to put on that morning. And it wasn't like this was a job interview or anything.

Only it felt like that. Like a job interview. But one where I didn't know what the position would entail or what qualifications I was meant to demonstrate to get it.

I mean, I was pretty sure I wasn't qualified for it. But other than that, my emotions were roiling like the high seas.

"It's going to be okay," Steph said. But again, the emotions that those words sparked in me—in this case, relief—were quickly dispelled by his next words. "He mainly wants to talk to you about what you did to that magical barrier in Geneva."

"But I don't even know what I did," I said.

Steph just gave me another reassuring smile. And I really hated how well those smiles worked on me. "It's just a conversation. Not an interrogation. Are you ready now?"

I chewed at my lip, but I couldn't find it in me to say no. "I just have to turn the sign back to *closed*," I said.

Steph raised a finger in the air and spun it around in a quick circle. "Done," he said.

"Show off," I grumbled, but I wasn't really mad. I picked up Houdini and held him close to my chest, then found myself once more tucked in close at Steph's side under the folds of that robe.

Butterscotch, rich and sweet, melting on my tongue.

But then the teleportation itself was over so quickly I scarcely felt it. I just blinked, and I was in a different, darker space.

It took a moment for my eyes to adjust. Not that the bookshop was ever very bright, not even at noon. But we had been in my nook, close to the south-facing window that looked out over the prosaic streets of Minneapolis.

Now we were in a space with no sunlight, no windows, and apparently no electricity. There were a few dim globules of light that I took for gas lamps until my vision finally adapted enough to make out the details.

They were magic lanterns, because of course they were. But unlike the arcane lights that Volumnia used to light her catacombs as well as the lantern she took out on her night-time wanderings, they weren't an eerie shade of green. No, they had a warm glow to them, actually a little more reminiscent of a wood fire than the gas lamps I had taken them for. I wondered if it was possible to turn them up higher.

Did Steph spend his time reading in light like this? Because if he did, he was going to be blind by forty for sure.

Once I could make out the lights, the other details started to emerge. We were standing in what looked like a front hall, only there was no sign of any door. A runner carpet extended from the bottom of a spiraling stone staircase in front of us to a featureless stone wall just at our backs.

That wall was bare, but the others were all covered in various tapestries, paintings, and brass sculptures that looked more like modern prosaic wall art than anything arcane.

"The Wizard gets a lot of catalogs," Steph said, practicing his old habit of seeming to read my mind. "He's loved mail order since it was invented. And he really likes internet shopping."

"Does he really never get out?" I asked. Not that I could imagine a wizard shopping in a mall or anything like that. Although I had to remind myself that I still didn't know what the Wizard looked like. And looking at his taste in art, I felt like I wanted to revise the mental image I'd already formed of him based on other wizards I had known in my academy days.

Although to what, I wasn't exactly sure.

"Tabitha, can you put me down?" Houdini asked.

"Certainly," I said, and set him down on the floor. But then I found myself running my hand over the lush scarlet carpet. The pile was so thick, it felt like it had just been installed. But it didn't have that new carpet smell. In fact, the only smell I could discern in that hall was a faint hint of dust, although there was no dust in sight anywhere around me.

Dust, but also books. I smelled books. Not in the hall, and not in either of the two adjoining rooms I could see opening onto the hall at the bottom of the stairs, but somewhere nearby.

"I would show you the way to the Wizard's private study, but it's just on the far side of the library," Steph said. "And somehow, I don't think you need my help to find that."

I smiled at him, enjoying the challenge. Then, Houdini close at my heels, I walked to the base of the stairs. The rooms to either side were in darkness, but one smelled of bread and herby stew, so I mentally labeled that one the kitchen. The other had an even fainter smell, like a fireplace that hadn't seen use in some time. Which, given it was August, made sense.

I labeled it the sitting room, since the "family" part of family room didn't really feel like it applied.

Then I headed up the stairs. The nails of Houdini's little paws made little skritching noises as we climbed. Steph, hands in his pockets and an amused expression on his face, trailed after.

The spiral of the stairs turned a complete circle, then joined with another hallway directly over the first. This one had four doors off of it, just visible in the dim light from the magic globes that stood one over each door. But all the doors were closed.

"Bedrooms?" I guessed, looking back at Steph.

"Bedrooms," he confirmed.

And I continued on through another complete spiral of the stairs to yet another hallway. Another four doors, all closed. But this time I was stumped. I turned to look at Steph.

"Workshops, mostly," he said. "The Wizard usually has master artisans create anything special that he needs for his work or studies. But sometimes he still chooses to work with his hands. Not as often as he would like, I think."

"And you? Do you like working with your hands?" I asked.

"Not in the workshop sense," he said, sliding an arm around my waist to pull me closer into a kiss.

"Shall I continue on my own?" Houdini asked testily.

"No, we're coming," I said. But gave Steph one last kiss before once more leading the way up the stairs.

A final turning, but I knew by the light that illuminated each step ahead of me more than the last that we weren't approaching yet another darkened hallway.

No, where we ended up was a massive circular room. There were stone walls all around us, but they were almost impossible to see. Not that the room was too dark; this space was the very opposite of dim despite the complete lack of windows.

There were just too many books around me to see much of anything beyond them. Books on shelves, and scrolls in racks, and stacks of loose paper on a variety of desks and tabletops. I was literally surrounded by books.

I drew in a deep breath, filling my lungs with the scents of leather and paper, vellum and ink, with soft undertones of musty dampness that was being held at bay, if not completely eradicated.

"I knew you'd love it," Steph said. But there was something different in his voice now than before. I turned to look at him, studying the dark brown eyes that were having such trouble meeting mine.

"You're nervous," I said at last, not quite an accusation. "Why are you nervous?"

"No reason," he said, too breezily. "This is going to be fine. Come on. The study is at the far end of the Tower."

The random arrangement of the bookshelves and scroll racks didn't lend itself to forming any kind of aisle, but Steph picked out a more or less straight path through it all, away from the stairs.

I looked down at Houdini. "Ready?" I asked him. I kind of hoped he would say no. I would've loved an excuse to hesitate, if only for a moment.

But his voice was firm in my mind. "Ready."

So I just nodded, fisted and unfisted my hands a few times,

wished again that I had worn something else, then took a final centering breath.

My only consolation was that if I ever someday met Steph's actual parents, there was no way it could ever be as stressful as this particular moment.

Then I hurried to catch up with Steph.

CHAPTER

SIXTEEN

The Wizard's private study wasn't so much a separate room as a space set apart from the rest of the library, where the haphazard arrangement of the bookshelves suddenly gained a sense of order. Not that the area was remotely squared off. It wasn't. The back wall was the outer wall of the Tower, and so had a curve to it. There was a fireplace at the midpoint that seemed to be nestled in that curve of stone wall. It would probably make the space before it quite cozy, if it were lit.

The rest of the space was defined by bookshelves that, while more than a dozen feet tall, didn't reach more than halfway up to the Tower ceiling far above us. And, like I said, they weren't remotely squared off. If anything, they had a sort of star-like arrangement to them. If I were to climb up into the heavy timber rafters high above where I was standing, it might look a little like the sort of star pattern that would be used on a quilt. At least until it reached that curve of stone wall.

The interior was not quite as cluttered as the library we had just picked our path through, but that was only by comparison. There were still a dozen desks and tables of various sizes, all covered in open tomes, scraps of parchment, alchemical equipment—some of which was actively bubbling and moving through glassware as we came in—and even a prosaic microscope that looked quite expensive and state-of-the-art to my admittedly untrained eye.

In the far corner off to my right, a cast-iron spiral staircase wound its way up past the tops of the bookshelves and beyond the heavy timber rafters to disappear in the shadows above. Although I couldn't see it, I reckoned there was a hatch there that led up to the roof of the Tower. Because, while there were numerous star charts hanging from the stone wall of the Tower behind a table cluttered with even more charts and no less than a dozen astrolabes of various sizes, there was no sign of a telescope in this study. But, then again, there were no windows either. To see the stars, you would have to go up on the roof. Hence the staircase.

As much as I loved my little nook in the bookshop, I had the strong urge to spend every waking minute in this space, exploring all the books and scrolls and studying samples under that microscope. And I had to imagine that magic was employed up on the roof to make it possible to see all the stars despite the fact that we were practically in the heart of Minneapolis.

"Sir?" Steph said, and I realized that while I had stopped following him the minute I had crossed the threshold, he, too, had come to a halt in the middle of the room. I looked around more carefully, trying to tune out all the fascinating details I wanted to dig into and only looking for any sign of the Wizard.

Not that I knew what he looked like. We had never met. But as far as I could tell, there was no one in the study but Steph, Houdini and me.

"He knew we were coming?" I said.

"He sent me to fetch you now specifically," Steph said, slowly turning in place as he looked around with a worried scowl. "I wasn't gone that long, but maybe he was summoned away while I was gone."

"Wouldn't that mean he could be anywhere?" I asked.

Steph gave me a helpless shrug. Houdini crossed the room to stand beside Steph's ankle as if to lend him emotional support.

But I found myself losing my inner battle to maintain focus. In the blink of an eye, I found myself standing at the high table before that modern microscope. I didn't quite have the courage to touch it, but I did look over all the drawings I could see on the pages of the open books and loose scraps of parchment before me. They all seemed to be different sorts of fungi, at least as I recalled studying such things in my mycology classes back in my academy days.

I was just leaning closer to one book to read the tiny captions on one of the drawings, hands carefully clasped together behind my back, when a voice behind me said, "I was, indeed, summoned away. But only by my own stomach, and only so far as the kitchen. Really, Stephanos, you jump so quickly to the most worrisome of conclusions."

I turned to see a stooped old man standing in the open space that served as a doorway between two bookshelves, a plate with a half-eaten sandwich on it gripped tightly in two arthritically twisted hands.

Well, stooped didn't quite cover it. He looked like in his youth he would've stood over six feet, but as the passing decades became passing centuries, he had sort of shrunk in on himself. The top of his head couldn't be more than five feet off the ground now, but those six feet of bones were still all there. They just jutted out now in protruding elbows and knees and the pronounced curvature of his spine. And all of those joints were knobby, but especially the knuckles of his hands.

Yet nothing stuck out more than his ears. His thin white hair was long, falling well past his shoulder blades in the back, but it parted around those ears, not even trying to cover them. They stood out in a way that I wanted to call elfin, but in the end I had to admit they weren't elegant enough for a Tolkien elf. No, they were more like the kind of ears you'd see on a troll doll. The kind with the super fuzzy, pastel hair.

"Ah, I see you're admiring my microscope," he said to me with a smile so wide, I momentarily stopped noticing his ears. "The prosaic world does excel at some things, don't they? Although I confess that's not my favorite thing they create."

"What is your favorite thing?" I asked, still clutching my hands behind my back.

The Wizard didn't answer, just turned the plate in his hands a quarter turn. But that was enough for me to see the stack of potato chips beside his sandwich. The distinctively hyperbolic paraboloid shape of those chips was, indeed, unique to the prosaic world.

"I love those, too," I admitted. "Probably a little too much."

He just gave me another smile, then continued across the room, sweeping past Steph to set the plate down on a small table beside a pair of reading chairs that stood close to the cold fireplace. He took one of the chips and crunched it thoughtfully as he looked first at me and then at Houdini.

"Master Houdini. I apologize for taking so long to make your acquaintance, but it was necessary to be absolutely sure it was safe to do so. Our dear Agatha went to such great efforts to keep you safe, I wasn't willing to take the risk of destroying all the protections she had given so much to create," he said. Then he settled himself down in a low squat, an alarming thing to watch someone of his age do. And it didn't exactly go smoothly. But when I looked to Steph in alarm, he subtly waved me off from rushing forward to help.

Not that he didn't look a little worried himself. But I got the sense that the Wizard didn't like to be fussed over.

It took the assistance of one of those reading chairs to do it, but the Wizard eventually got to where he was sitting on his haunches more or less comfortably. Then he held out one of those permanently curled, knobby-knuckled hands out to Houdini.

Houdini trotted forward at once and let the old man touch his head without a single word of warning about not touching his ears. Houdini hated being touched by strangers, and was slow to take people out of that category, but apparently the Wizard wasn't bound by the normal rules.

"I understand the delicacy of the situation well, sir," Houdini said with a slight bow of his head. "I, more than anyone, do not wish to see Agatha's sacrifice be in vain."

"Yes, of course. Although it's not always easy, being the thing that has to be protected, is it?" the Wizard said.

"No, it is not," Houdini said. But he sounded pleased that the Wizard understood him so well. "You and Agatha were friends?"

"I don't think that is the word she would have used," the Wizard said musingly. "Nor I, either. Sometimes it felt closer to enemies, especially in our younger days. But time softened the edges of both our personalities, I think."

I almost choked out loud at that. The Agatha I had known had been the furthest thing from soft.

But it didn't take much to imagine a sharper version of her in her youth. Actually, I suddenly wanted a lot more details on what she had been like when she had been a witch my own age. Did any of the books and journals she had left to Audrey go that far back in time? I'd have to remember to ask the next time I saw Audrey.

"There is one thing I would like to understand," Houdini said, still speaking in his most formal voice in our minds.

"Please, ask," the Wizard said, even as he used the arm of the reading chair to slowly get back to his feet, then half-sit, half-collapse down into it as if suddenly exhausted.

Houdini waited until this was done, then hopped up to sit on the cushion of the opposite chair before asking, "I know the magical pull of your Tower is what brought me here when I was born, but from what I've read that would take very old magic. Very old. And yet the Square only goes back a century and a half."

"Yes, very astute of you," the Wizard said. He put the plate of food on his lap and picked off a bit of the sandwich. I could smell tuna and dill pickles, and more faintly caraway from the bread as he crumbled it. He put the world's smallest bite into his mouth, as if stalling for time to think.

"Agatha was the strongest power in the creation of the Square, wasn't she?" Houdini asked.

"Yes. Yes, she was," the Wizard said. "This place called to her, but in a way she would never describe to me. She just felt like she belonged here. But once she had the basic wards around this place and was certain the prosaic neighborhood was trained to grow around it properly, she extended an invitation for me to join her. And so I did."

"Trained to grow?" I asked.

"Like beans up a pole or ivy up a trellis," the Wizard said. "The local people don't realize they are being guided in their building if you do it properly. They just make the most logical decisions for their own wellbeing, and if you've set up your infrastructure correctly, those decisions lead them on the path that also serves your own needs."

"The garden metaphor is deliberate," Steph told me. "It's more of a symbiotic relationship that serves everyone's needs."

"As opposed to?" I asked.

"Some wizards see themselves more as architects, with prosaics being their raw materials, to be used as required for the job," the Wizard said with clear distaste. "Those communities, not surprisingly, seldom last long."

"But the Tower," Houdini pressed.

"Yes, the Tower," the Wizard said, tearing another tiny bite off his sandwich. "This place has been my home for longer than most can imagine. I won't tell you precisely the time involved, neither will I tell you where it originally stood. Know only that when Agatha extended her invitation, and I took it, I put considerable effort into bringing it over here from its original location. It took more than a decade to get all the spells in place to preserve its power and root it to grow again in this bedrock. More than a decade, and more than twelve wizards assisted me in the process. But here it is, and here it thrives."

Then he set the plate of food aside to lean forward in his chair, putting his face close to Houdini's. "Now, let's take a look at you."

"Can you see me?" Houdini asked, sitting up a little taller on the chair and blinking in surprise. "I mean, really see me?"

"No, I'm afraid I cannot," the Wizard said. "Not even in this place, where my magic is strongest. No, thanks to Agatha's magic, even I see only a little black dog with strangely intelligent eyes."

"No aura or shimmer or anything?" Steph asked, drawing closer behind the Wizard's shoulder as if he, too, wanted a better look at Houdini.

"Not even a hint," the Wizard said, as if that fact delighted him. He reached out to touch the collar around Houdini's neck. "This has a glow, but there is magic in here that Agatha did not do herself."

"Audrey and I added some things," I said, for the very first time wondering if that had been a mistake. What if trying to help had messed up what Agatha had already done?

"Yes, I see two threads of power in these spells," the Wizard said in that musing tone of voice again. He seemed to be stroking the air around the collar rather than the collar itself, and Houdini looked a little unnerved. But then the Wizard sat back in his chair, elbows on the armrests as he steepled his knobby fingers under his chin. "Few wizards so young have the knack for what you two did. The total spell is stronger than the sum of its parts. It's not Agatha level, of course. Not even close. Still, it shows promise. Working effectively in a team is a skill too few emerging from our academies seem to ever acquire."

I swallowed nervously, but couldn't help saying, "Well, Audrey and I aren't remotely wizards. We barely even pass as witches, sir."

"You're better at assessing that than I am, are you?" he said, giving me a sharp look. But there was still the hint of a smile at the corners of his mouth.

"No, sir," I said. "But I've been assessed a lot, and it's never come out well."

The Wizard chuckled at that, but whatever he was thinking that so amused him, he didn't speak it out loud.

"You are safe enough, young dragon," the Wizard said to Houdini. "If I can't see your true nature, I feel confident enough to say no one can. But even so, now that you've been inside the Tower, it will always be open to you. If you ever feel yourself in danger, this place will be your sanctuary."

"Thank you, sir," Houdini said with another little bow of his head. "But if you can't see my dragon nature, does that mean you can't see what kind of dragon I am?"

"I'm afraid not, little one," the Wizard said. "Not just by looking, anyway. But Steph assures me he is still working hard to find out anything that can be known. I know it's frustrating when such things take time, especially for the young. But if I've learned anything in all my years, it's that time passes. It may feel fast or slow, but it always passes. And answers that can only come in time feel like they are always too far away. But they will come."

"Then I shall try to be patient," Houdini said. But my heart wanted to break a little at the sound of discouragement in his tone. I wanted to pick him up and cuddle him close. To give him every comfort I could.

But before I could so much as make a move, the Wizard was looking at me. Even in the semidarkness of the book-lined room, his eyes stood out brightly as they locked with mine. They were like shining emeralds, completely untouched by the time that had done such damage to the rest of his body.

"Now, Miss Tabitha Greene. It's time to take a look at you."

CHAPTER

SEVENTEEN

It was hard in that moment not to have flashbacks of my last job interview. You know, the one where I had set one of my potential employers on fire when asked to demonstrate just a little magic.

There was a dry lump in my throat I couldn't swallow down, but I did manage to force my feet to move, to cross the room to the chair opposite of where the Wizard sat. Houdini got up on his back legs, raising his front legs towards me. He can hold that pose for a length of time that would make you think he was bucking for a position as a circus dog. But I scooped him up, sat in his place, and settled him on my lap.

Then I had no clue what to do next.

The Wizard was sitting back in his chair again, resting his chin on his steepled index fingers. I couldn't guess what thoughts or feelings lurked behind those green eyes; they were completely inscrutable.

And for the longest time, he didn't say anything. But the only thing I was one hundred percent sure about was that I had to let him be the one to speak first.

It was the hardest thing in the world.

But when my eyes briefly flicked up to Steph still standing behind the Wizard's shoulder, the look on his face was clear as day. It said, "You've got this."

So I just petted the soft hair of Houdini's back and waited.

Nothing in the Wizard's position had shifted at all, not the expressionless mask of his face or the posture of his body. So when he finally spoke, the words felt like they came out of nowhere. "Do you know what it is that I study?"

"Study?" I said, as if I'd forgotten the meaning of the word in the meager few weeks since I had left my last magical academy. "You mean, like, research?"

He nodded.

"No. But, to be honest, it looks like a little bit of everything," I said, glancing around at all the cluttered tables and desks around us. His eyes darted around, too, as if he'd forgotten the details of the room around us until I had called his attention to it.

"Most of this is work I do at the request of others," he said. "I meant my passion. The thing I feel such a longing to understand that I find every morning that I simply must live another day, if only to learn just a little more."

"Oh," I said, a little disoriented as my mind ran in two different directions at once.

Part of me was still trying to figure out the answer to his question.

But another part of me was trying to figure out what *that* had meant. It sounded like, without the call of endless research and study, he would no longer have the drive to keep living. Which, granted, he was centuries old. I didn't know how old, but I knew it was *old* old. And even in the magical world, that was a rare thing.

I could certainly easily imagine the pull of knowledge to be gained being enough to get me out of bed every morning for an eternity.

But Agatha had been impossibly old as well. And she had shown no interest in such things. And I didn't think she'd had any interests like that even before she'd compromised so much of her own magic for the sake of protecting Houdini.

I could feel the weight of the Wizard's gaze on me, and forced my mind back to just the one track of thought. But in the end I had to shake my head. I couldn't even guess.

"It *is* a little esoteric," Steph said, as much to me as to the Wizard. "They don't teach it in any of the schools."

"They ought to," the Wizard said.

"What would they teach?" Steph asked in a perfectly reasonable tone of voice. But I got the sense this was an old topic between them.

"Someday they'll teach what I learn," the Wizard said, as close as I'd heard him yet to sounding grumpy. But then his attention was back on me. "I study spacetime. It's been an interest of mine since I formed a friendship of sorts with a prosaic man by the name of Isaac Newton."

"I've certainly heard of him," I said.

"Yes, I'm sure you have. You have an impressively broad range in your reading material," the Wizard said. I didn't know how to respond to that. But I didn't have to ask how he knew that. The tinge of color to Steph's cheeks gave that answer away.

But the Wizard was still speaking, and I brought my eyes back to meet his. "Space and time are not separate things. They are interrelated. The finest prosaic minds know this, but, of course, they don't understand how any of it pertains to magic. Not that I do myself, but I am studying it."

"Are you trying to create a new branch of magic? One that draws from spacetime rather than nature or ritual or what have you?" I asked, keenly interested. I had tried every branch of magic they taught in the academies, for greater or lesser lengths of time. And I had failed at them all.

But I hadn't even thought of branches that *weren't* taught. I mean, aside from the outright evil ones like necromancy, which, I would never.

"Not as such. At least, not yet," the Wizard said. There was an eager flame in his eyes, the sign of the passion that still got him up every morning, eager to get back to work.

"But that wasn't really your point," Steph said.

"No, you're right," the Wizard said, giving him the barest of nods of thanks for getting him back on track before he got well and truly distracted. "What I was trying to get across is that the dichotomy I have studied for so many years, space and time, isn't really a dichotomy at all."

"Okay," I said, but I wasn't getting his point at all, really.

A fact I knew he could tell, as he gave me a soft smile. "All of which is just preamble to admitting that your problem is outside of my expertise."

"The Wizard is highly competent in all sorts of spheres that are outside of his expertise," Steph said, faster than I could even register any disappointment at the Wizard's words.

"If I weren't, I would be a poor candidate for training an apprentice such as yourself, wouldn't I?" the Wizard groused. I expected Steph to look chagrined at being dressed down like that. It took me a minute to realize the glow on his cheeks was from the compliment very carefully hidden in those words.

"So my... magic is not your chosen field of study, but you're still as knowledgeable in it as any other living wizard," I said. I had hesitated only for the barest fractions of a second before deciding not to name my type of magic, but the Wizard heard it all the same.

"We are free to speak here, Tabitha," he said. "No one else may know what is said or done inside these walls. You may trust in that, just as Houdini may. This is a safe space, even for chaos magic as powerful as yours."

"I didn't mean to bring those wards down in Geneva," I said, and that lump was back in my throat. Only this time it was a wet lump.

"No, I could see that you did not," the Wizard said, his eyes half-closed as if summoning the memory back in a way only he could see. "You wanted to save the books."

"Well, the books, and our lives," I admitted.

"Whatever your intent, the act itself is what matters," the Wizard said, and I braced myself for the sort of lectures about consequences I had gotten so many times before in my academy days.

I had started a lot of fires. Never on purpose. But, as I was all too aware, intent didn't really matter if the alchemy wing burned to the ground because of something I did.

The Wizard was watching me closely, as if all the memories running through my mind were also running across my face like it was a movie screen.

Then he said, "In this case, the act preserved the rest of the magical community in Geneva."

"It what?" I asked, not sure I had heard him correctly.

"Oh, yes," the Wizard said, and shifted in his chair to look up at Steph's equally surprised face. "It's not the best design, the interconnected pockets of Geneva. One large community and many small, individual communities have their pros and cons, of course. But the interconnected small communities always combine the worst of both without the advantages of either."

"Yes," Steph said, but as if only halfway through the process of calling up some forgotten fact from his education. He tapped at his lip with one thumbnail until he had it. "That's why the Square isn't connected to the rest of the hidden city under Minneapolis."

"But, the water tunnels," I said. Because I had, on more than one occasion, taken a magic boat through the tunnel that plunged under the Mississippi River, to the buildings that magic folk lived in under downtown.

"Those are connections only in the mundane sense," the Wizard said with a dismissive wave.

"He's taking about the warding," Steph told me. "The wards that protect and hide this place are separate from the rest of Minneapolis." Then he glanced down at the Wizard as if for permission to speak before adding, "That was why the Wizard agreed to move here when Agatha invited him to come. Because her design was safer."

"But didn't I ruin it in Geneva when I pulled it down?" I asked.

"You exposed that pocket, but it was burned to ash before the prosaics could safely look at any of it," the Wizard said. "They didn't even find a body, let alone the remains of any magical text. It was all perfectly safe."

I was momentarily overwhelmed, thinking of all the books that were now lost forever. Most of it probably still existed in other copies or other forms, somewhere in the world.

But not all of it. Something I couldn't even imagine had been lost to the world for good. Maybe a couple of somethings.

I felt the loss, only made more acute for not knowing exactly what I was mourning.

"You cut that pocket off from the rest of the warding," the Wizard said. "Before the prosaics came in, which they surely would have. Fighting fire is just the sort of powerful motivator that always brings our protections down. The prosaics were going to come in through those walls, whether the wards were up or down. Taking them down when you did didn't change that. But it did secure the wards that protected the adjacent pockets of magical Geneva."

"It's like a hole in a knit sweater," Steph said. "Instead of loose threads unraveling everything, you pulled the rest of the knitting tighter around it and closed up the hole. It's all perfectly secure now. It won't unravel any further."

"Oh," I said, feeling a little numb. I couldn't quite wrap my mind around what they were telling me. "I mean, I didn't know I could even do that, or that I should try to do that, or any of it. I just... wanted to make it rain."

"You wanted to protect things," the Wizard said. "With all your heart. And that's what the magic did for you."

"That doesn't sound particularly chaotic, though," I said. I realized I had stopped petting Houdini, who appeared to have gone to sleep on my lap anyway. Instead, I was twisting that silver bracelet around and around on my wrist.

"Doesn't it?" the Wizard said, almost sounding amused. "You couldn't do what you wanted to do. And if you had tried harder to do what you intended, you would've only not done it harder. So to speak."

"We don't really understand how chaos works, of course," Steph said, as much to the Wizard as to me.

"We know that the world needs chaos to function as much as it needs order," the Wizard said. "Order is too rigid. Too inflexible and unchanging. Too concerned with micromanaging. Chaos, and particularly chaos with something like your heart behind it, is just the sort of big, messy upheaval that is so necessary for progress."

"But isn't order magic just as mysterious as chaos magic, because all the texts on it were destroyed?" I asked.

"It exists, but it's not understood the way it should be," the Wizard said. But he was looking suddenly tired, pressing a hand to his forehead. That hand was trembling, if only ever so slightly.

"I wish we hadn't lost that book," I said.

"We'll find it," Steph said, firmly resolute.

"Well, perhaps," the Wizard said, rubbing at his eyes before dropping that hand. He looked at the plate of food on the table beside him as if surprised to see so much sandwich still sitting there, uneaten. But then he turned back to me, his gaze still so intent I wanted to squirm in my chair. "The book is not necessary to begin training you in control. Although, from what I've seen in Geneva, you aren't going to need anywhere near as much training as I had initially thought."

"Really?" I said. I didn't feel that way at all. I still felt like if he took my silver bracelet away, I'd instantly be a fire risk again.

"Oh, it will still be arduous enough for you, I'm sure," he said with a dry little laugh. "Practically everything seems to happen in no time at all to me now, with all my years behind me. But it will feel different for you." But that burst of amusement was gone as quickly as it had come, and a sense of melancholy seemed to radiate from the Wizard's entire body.

"We should go," Steph said, and I nodded. Houdini woke up at once and hopped to the floor, shaking his whole body in that way he did every time he woke from a nap, no matter how brief.

But I hesitated before taking Steph's hand.

"Did you tell him about the blackmail?" I asked Steph, in a whisper that the Wizard heard perfectly well.

"I appreciate your concern, Tabitha Greene," the Wizard said with a tired attempt at his earlier smile. "But I assure you, I fear nothing of that sort. The kinds of secrets I fear getting out into the world are not the kind of secrets that would ever have found their way into that safe. You need not worry on my account."

I wasn't quite sure how to respond to that. Not that it mattered. Steph had me on my feet and on my way out of the study too fast for me to get out more than a hasty thanks and goodbye.

Then, in the blink of an eye, we were back in my nook in the bookshop. And for the third time that week, I was startled to see the sun still up.

"We're still going to find that book," Steph promised me. "One way or another, we'll find it."

"The Wizard didn't seem to think it was so very important," I said. But I wasn't sure how I felt about it at all.

"Someone murdered Prospero Talbot to get their hands on it," Steph said. "I know little things like theft and murder have a hard time sinking in for the Wizard. There is a downside to living so long. He loses the sort of context for that stuff that the rest of us can't help but feel in our bones. It might not be important to the history of magic a couple of centuries from now, but it's important to us? Right?"

"Right," I said. I could certainly agree to that much. But I was feeling something else even more strongly. "But if it wasn't about the book, if it was about the blackmail, I want to know that too. Not the salacious details, obviously. I want to know who killed Prospero Talbot and why, even if it wasn't about the book in the end."

"I know you do," Steph said, and kissed me.

Somewhere, in the back of my mind, I heard Houdini make a groan objecting to the public display of affection.

But it was one I easily tuned out.

CHAPTER

EIGHTEEN

Houdini and I were running late the next morning, reaching the Loose Leaves Teashop too late to help set the table for breakfast. Even Barnardo had beaten us down, already sitting in his customary chair and chatting with Liam as Audrey poured out the tea.

I was momentarily distracted by the bergamot scent, always a sign for her most strongly caffeinated blend. Which was exactly what I needed that morning, after a sleepless night plagued by nightmares of fire and burning books. Those nightmares had been intense, as if making up for missing me the first night after the actual fire.

So it wasn't until Houdini asked me, "Where is Miss Snooty Cat?" that I realized our little breakfast party was short more than the elusive Steph.

"Yes, where is Miss Snooty Cat?" I asked out loud as I slipped into my chair. Barnardo gave me a puzzled look, but only because of how I had started that sentence with a "Yes."

"She had some things to do on her own, I guess," he said with a shrug.

"She's more a companion than a pet to you, isn't she?" Audrey said as she set the teapot down on its little warmer and draped a towel over it snugly while it steeped.

"Oh, I would never call her a pet," Barnardo said with a nervous laugh, as if afraid that Miss Snooty Cat might overhear him and come to the wrong conclusion. "I don't think even my father ever considered her his pet."

"So she was your father's...?" I trailed off, still not sure what the word was that Barnardo wasn't saying.

"She was with my father for five years," Barnardo said as he buttered a scone. "Just turned up one day outside his apartment door looking for food. He let her in and fed her, and she never really left again. I sort of inherited her after my father died. But we'd been together for months before that. I moved back home to take care of him, you know. About a year ago now. I used to live downtown."

"In Minneapolis?" I said. This was news to me.

"Yes. Not in the hidden floors of the Foshay Tower or anything so swank as that, but downtown. A nice enough place. But I didn't mind giving it up to come back to the Square, really. This place has always been my home." He took a hefty bite from his herby scone, sending a cascade of crumbs down onto his plate.

"So Miss Snooty Cat had somewhere else to be this morning?" I said before nibbling on a corner of my own scone. Carefully, having seen how crumbly they were. But not carefully enough. Unlike Barnardo, I ended up with crumbs scattering over my lap.

"I assume so," he said with a shrug. "She'll be back when she's back. I don't poke around in her business."

I looked around for Houdini to see what he made of this, but he was clear across the room, chomping on a plate of treats that Audrey had left out for him.

"These are amazing," Houdini said. I nearly laughed out loud. It made no sense why the voice that spoke directly in the back of my mind should so convincingly conveying him speaking with his mouth full. But it did.

Audrey had a napkin over her mouth, hiding her own smile, so I knew it wasn't just me.

"Those are peanut butter and bacon," Liam said. "Sounds a little iffy to me, but he sure seems to be enjoying them."

Houdini looked up at us as he chewed the last of his third treat, looking for all the world like an internet video of an otter enjoying a snack. If he was worried about what Miss Snooty Cat was up to, he certainly wasn't showing it.

But was it worrisome, really? If she was off doing her own thing, that probably meant she was doing just what she promised to do: find out more about Houdini's background and family. If she could. Which was still a big if in my mind. But I'd rather she tried and failed honestly than that she was conning Houdini somehow.

"No news from Geneva, then?" Audrey asked all of us at the table.

"Nothing from me," I said. Which wasn't exactly true, but what the Wizard had said about the wards could wait until later, when it was just the two of us.

"There was an interesting arc to the chatter yesterday, for sure," Barnardo said. "Rumors were spreading like wildfire until later in the afternoon, and then everything sort of died out."

"Like a hush campaign of some kind?" I asked, not liking the sound of *that* at all.

But Barnardo just gave another careless shrug. "Maybe? When names like Manx and Ward get thrown around, hush campaigns or outright questionable use of that sort of magic are always possibilities. But this is more like once all the stories ran the circuit, there was nothing more to add. No one really knows what any of the blackmail material might have been, if it even existed at all. There's no real sense of who specifically in those families was targeted, let alone for what. And when it was clear that no one really knew anything, the mills just ground to a stop."

"I guess it's good no one is making things up to keep the stories going, anyway," Liam said.

"Well, nothing was found at the site of the fire, even when the magical authorities went over it after the prosaics had gone," Barnardo said. "I mean, they had already taken care of the body, but any hope that they'd find more evidence later didn't pan out. And no one has seen hide nor hair of the brother, so..." He trailed off with another shrug.

"Any word on your end about the brother?" I asked Liam.

"Only what I told you yesterday," Liam said, but pulled out his phone to double check his feeds. He scrolled for a minute, then shook his head. "Nope. Just reprinting what they said yesterday. With a few extra details about his past, but most of what I told you yesterday is only now starting to come to light. So you're still ahead of the game."

"Well, that's definitely not how it feels," I said. "I feel behind. No, I feel like the game is taking place on an entirely different continent, and I'm pretty far removed from all of it."

"That's true, too," Barnardo said with a teasing smile.

"Well, if you were looking for something to do in the meantime, there's always that spell to help me," Liam said.

"Sorry, I really didn't get much pulled together yesterday," I admitted. "And today might not be great. I didn't sleep well. My brain is running on fumes, and I really need it to get into proper research mode. But this helps," I added, saluting Audrey with my teacup.

"Oh, sure. No rush," Liam said. But he couldn't be less convincing at being casual about it.

"I know it's important to you," I assured him. "I just want to give it my best shot."

He nodded and turned his attention back to his scone.

I wished I could find the right words to tell him without hurting his feelings that as cool as magic seemed to him now, relying on it for everything was never a great idea. And relying on it for things like a job search in the prosaic world really felt like the wrong tool for the job. But I hadn't been joking about my lack of brain function. The tea was doing its job, but there was a limit to what it could do when what was really needed was another four or so hours of proper sleep.

Barnardo was just reminiscing about one of the blackmail rumors that he was pretty sure didn't have a grain of truth to it, but felt compelled to share with the rest of us anyway when Liam's phone resting facedown on the table buzzed loudly.

"Sorry!" Liam said, snatching it up at once. Barnardo carried on with his story, but I shifted my chair a little closer to try to sneak a peek at Liam's phone. I couldn't read the text, but I recognized the photo as the burned remains of the Talbot Book Repository.

"What does it say?" I asked in a whisper. But even that was enough to interrupt Barnardo's story. Well, that, and the fact that only Audrey was still putting up the pretense of listening to gossip about people we didn't even know.

"Tell us," Barnardo prompted as Liam looked from his phone to each of us and then back to his phone again.

"The brother. Antonio Talbot. He's officially been declared a person of interest in the case," Liam said.

"By the prosaic authorities?" I asked. "But how do they know he's even involved? They didn't find the body, and they don't know the name of the bookshop. Do they?"

"No, it's still only identified as arson of an abandoned building that may once have been a church," he said, still tapping and scanning on his phone. "But there is a clear shot of his face on the CCTV cameras in the area. On a couple of them, actually, both before and after the time they suspect the fire was started."

"But lots of people must've walked by those cameras," I said, flushing as I realized that I myself was one of those people.

"Well, he does have a criminal record," Liam said.

"For arson?" Audrey asked.

"No, I don't think so," Liam said, frowning as he set down his phone, then reached for his notebook in the bag under his chair. He flipped through the pages until he found where he had taken notes about Antonio's background. "No, it was for panhandling and loitering, never for anything violent or destructive. But he would be in their databases just for being arrested."

"You said person of interest, not suspect, right?" I asked.

"Yeah," Liam said, but too slowly.

"One leads to the other, then," I guessed.

"If they were looking for a witness, they would be bringing a lot more people in," he said. "I mean, you're probably on these cameras too, right?"

"Yeah, but how would they know who I am?" I pointed out. So far as I knew, I didn't exist on any prosaic database. Not only had I never been fingerprinted or given a DNA sample of any kind, I didn't have a birth certificate or any other form of the usual identifications. In the prosaic world, I was a ghost.

But Antonio Talbot wasn't. He had taken all the steps to exist there. And now that choice was having a consequence.

We finished our breakfast without another alert on Liam's phone or any sign of Miss Snooty Cat. So Houdini and I had to make our way over to the bookshop to start the business day, with both of us wondering when we would know what was really going on in our separate quests.

Houdini curled up to nap in the dog bed under the apothecary desk, apparently resigned to his fate of waiting for news.

But I couldn't get myself to such a calmly patient place. I had to do... something.

Not that I knew what that something could possibly be. But I knew where I could start.

I called for Steph.

CHAPTER

NINETEEN

Steph appeared the instant I spoke his name out loud. Almost as if he had been waiting to hear from me. Which meant he probably could've made it to our breakfast meeting, but I decided not to bring that up.

Especially after I got a look at how pale and drawn his face was.

"Is something wrong?" I asked.

"No, no. It was just a long night," he said, and rubbed at his face tiredly. That brought a little color to his cheeks. But that color only highlighted the redness of his eyes.

"Did something happen? In Geneva or with the murder case?" I asked.

"No," he said, still sounding like he was trying to forcibly placate me to my ears. I expected him to deflect my questions harder, but all at once he just gave in with a weary sigh. "Here's the thing. I know what you saw yesterday was just the Wizard chatting with Houdini and then chatting with you—"

"Oh, I know it was more than that," I said. "He was looking at us both so intently. And I just don't think he declared the Tower safe for both of us—and I think also that we were safe to be in the Tower,

159

frankly—without any evidence. He was... I don't know. Scanning us?"

"He was," Steph said, clearly impressed that I had noticed that. "But it was more than that. You see, the reason he brought the Tower with him when he moved here from the Old World is that they are a symbiotic pair. He exists because it still does, and vice versa. Your presence, and Houdini's as well, put a certain tension on those bonds."

"Oh, dear," I said, horrified that I hadn't noticed *that* at all.

"Nothing bad," Steph rushed to clarify. "It was necessary, actually, for it to be a safe haven for the both of you. Which he wanted it to be. That's why he had invited you to call on him, just as soon as he'd laid the groundwork for that. But even with all that groundwork for weeks ahead of time, it's going to take him some time after to recover. It was a pretty major piece of magic, even invisible as it mostly was."

"He did seem to tire very quickly near the end there," I said, a bit embarrassed that I had chalked that up to his age. But at least I hadn't said so out loud. "But he's better today?"

"He's resting," Steph said.

"As you should be, from the looks of you," I said.

"No, I'm here for you now," he said. "I spent the night constantly repairing tears in the magical fabric of the Tower, but that's all done now. It's finished its structural modifications, and now it's just a matter of building back the power. That just takes time. Sleeping isn't going to make that happen faster."

"Sometimes sleep is its own reward," I said.

"Tabitha, you called me here, which you almost never do," he said. "Just tell me what you need."

"I don't *need* anything," I said.

"But—?"

"But I would *like* to go back to Geneva. If possible. To try to find Antonio Talbot before the prosaics do," I finally spit out.

"Antonio's apartment and place of employment both are pretty far from the magical parts of the city. Or, at least, as far as they can be, given that it's Geneva," Steph said.

"You know where he lives?" I asked.

"Liam gave me the addresses yesterday," he said. Which was news to me. I had no idea the two of them were meeting outside of our breakfasts.

The breakfasts Steph kept missing.

But he wasn't done talking. "I can bring us to the nearest portal, but it's still going to involve time on a prosaic bus, as well as some walking. And if there's trouble, that means being stranded far from a portal."

"Is that a problem?" I asked. "We weren't near a portal the first time we jumped to Europe."

"The Wizard has the robe at the moment, and he'll need it if he gets a summons. Because there's no way he'll tell the High Council that he's depleted. Even though he is, in fact, almost totally depleted."

"Maybe a different time, then," I said. "I don't like leaving him alone in such a state."

"No, I'm curious to speak to this brother as well," Steph said. "And the last thing the Wizard would want is for me to hang around fussing over him. Let me just send Houdini to keep an eye on him while we're gone."

He started to turn towards the apothecary desk—as if he already knew that's where Houdini was napping, out of sight—but spun back around to say one last thing to me. "You just have to promise me if anything so much as feels off, we back away. Because running away on foot is going to have to be our first line of defense. We'll be completely in the prosaic world. We can't risk exposure."

"I get it," I said. "I'll let you make the call when we bail. Unless something flags my danger sense first. But anyway, I won't argue if you say it's time to go. Deal?"

"Deal," he said.

I felt a little guilty about closing the bookshop again, but it was still a weekday. So long as I made sure to be open over the weekend, I would still be there for the bulk of our prosaic walk-in customers.

Houdini walked with us as far as the entry to the hedge maze, then made his own way to the Tower. But I could tell by the jaunty angle of his corkscrew tail that he considered his task watching over the resting Wizard to be a high honor. He was clearly quite pleased with himself.

Then Steph and I jumped through the portal to the same familiar rooftop in Geneva. It was still early evening there, the sky low over the mountaintops to the west but not yet setting. The fried potato smell was as strong as ever, but the sounds of passing crowds and cars on the streets below were louder but less distinct, more a general urban hum than a collection of discreet noises now.

I had assumed I would have to take the lead in the prosaic world, but was quickly disabused of that notion when Steph took out his cellphone and called up a schedule for the local public transportation.

"Oh, good," he said as we jogged down the flights of stairs to reach street level. "Liam set us up with day passes on the local bus lines. We just have to scan a code when we get on board and not worry about the local money."

I pulled out my phone to see a text from Liam with a link for my own version of the app. I downloaded it as I followed Steph to the closest bus stop.

"Do you speak any French?" he asked as we waited for the bus.

"Mais oui," I said. "Ein bisschen Deutsch auch. If it comes up. How about you?"

"I can mangle my way through most of the Romance languages after all the Latin I learned for ritual magic. But it's not pretty," he said.

It took nearly an hour and two bus changes before we reached our destination, but Geneva was a gorgeous city, so it was hard to mind too terribly much. That, and sharing a narrow bus seat with Steph had its own distractions. But the sun was just beginning to set when we finally reached our stop. We got out with a crowd of eight other passengers, all clearly workers heading home for the night, as our stop was centrally located between four different apartment buildings.

"This one," Steph said, directing my attention to the tallest but shabbiest of the three. The elevator was out, but I was starting just to expect climbing stairs to be a part of my life these days. Even with all that practice lately, I was still sweating profusely by the time we reached the tenth floor.

We were both too winded to speak, although Steph was sort of aspirating the sounds of numbers as we passed door after door, looking for our destination.

We turned a corner, and Steph promptly stopped counting.

Because it would be way too much of a coincidence for the door not only standing open but hanging brokenly from a single hinge not to be our door.

"Do we rabbit?" I asked. I knew my heart rate, which had just started to come down after the stairs, was racing all over again.

But everything past that broken door just looked dark. Dark and empty.

Only the outside world we had left just minutes before had barely started turning to dusk. That apartment was too dark.

"No," Steph said after a long moment's thought. But he took out his wand before stepping closer to the door. I let him go first, but I stayed as close beside him as I could. For as much good as I could do.

We reached the doorway, but everything before us was impenetrable darkness. One I really didn't want to just walk into.

"Do you have a light spell handy?" I asked, not sure why I was whispering. If the neighbors had somehow missed the sound of the door being blown apart like that, the two of us talking was hardly going to raise alarm.

"Well," Steph said, giving me a sidelong grin. Then he reached forward into that darkness, but only far enough to find the light switch.

Two lamps flared to life. One stood on a heavy console on the far side of the room, the sort of console I suspected contained a very old television set behind those closed cabinet doors.

The other was closer to us, but lying on its side, its shade pushed askew, and the light from its bulb mostly lighting up the carpet around it.

Steph glanced around very briefly before putting his wand away. A decision that felt a little hasty to me. Although when he picked up the fallen lamp and put it back on the nearby end table it must've belonged on, the shadows in the corners of the room arranged themselves into a slightly less ominous configuration.

Then he crossed the room and pulled open the blackout curtains, filling the room with dim evening light. The view out of the window was almost impossible to make out through all the grime, but appeared to be nothing more than the wall of the facing apartment building as well as the windows in the adjacent units, far too close for comfort. The grime and the curtain made a lot more sense. Even as I crept up behind Steph to look out for myself, I saw a trio of young children in the apartment opposite of us shrieking and pointing at us.

"I'm not sensing residual magic here," Steph said as he turned away from the window.

"This doesn't look like messy living, though," I said as I bent to pick up a few of the books that were strewn over the floor in front of a homemade bookshelf made from cheap wood planks and cinderblocks. I looked at each of the titles, but nothing caught my eye.

"No, someone was here looking for something," Steph agreed as he moved around a half wall that separated the living space from a very rudimentary kitchen. There was a single door on the far side, but when he clicked on the light, all that was revealed was a bathroom so tiny the toilet was practically in the shower. And I wasn't sure how there was room to get inside and shut the door without plastering yourself against the none-too-clean walls.

"No bedroom?" I said, looking around for another door. But there wasn't one. I looked closer at the couch. It didn't pull out. But there was a basket tucked between it and the wall that had been filled with sheets and a thin blanket, now tossed around that corner of the room.

Steph whispered the words of a spell I didn't recognize. Suddenly, his eyes glowed softly with a golden light. Then he looked around the room again, slowly turning as his eyes swept over everything. Once he was facing the same position he had started in, he blinked hard and his eyes were back to normal.

"There's nothing here, but we should go," he said, reaching a hand out to me.

"I'm not done checking these books," I said, looking down at the pile I was still standing in the middle of. "Everything I've found so far is prosaic, but there's like two hundred books here. How did he even get them all to fit on those shelves?"

"Unorthodox shelving techniques," Steph said wryly. But then he was all seriousness again. "Tabitha, time to go."

"Right," I said with a sigh. I had given my word, after all. I set the books I still had in my hands on the shelves, then followed him back out of the apartment.

We headed back to the bus stop, and I sank gratefully down onto the bench to wait.

So many stairs.

Steph was checking the screen of his phone again.

"The bookstore where he works is pretty close to here, right?" I said.

"Yeah, but I'm not sure if there's much point in going there," Steph said. "Liam just sent me a news report from the local prosaic press. Antonio was spotted in Canada, of all places."

"That sounds a little improbable," I said. "They've been looking for him. How could he get out through an airport?"

"Unless he left before they started looking for him," Steph said.

"Yeah, but, they'd know that, right? They track those things. As soon as they started looking for him, they'd know if he took a flight to Canada," I said.

"If he took a prosaic flight, yes," Steph said. "But, as much as he's been living here for years by his own choice, we know for a fact he still has contacts in our world."

"You think Violenta Court is helping him?" I asked.

"Maybe not her, but there's nothing saying she's the only witch he's stayed in contact with, is there?" Steph asked.

"Do you think he still has the book?" I asked. "Did he bring it to Canada?"

"Perhaps he hopes to sell it there," Steph said. "I can look into more once we get back home."

Then he looked at the time on the screen of his phone and took a step out into the road to look for the bus.

But something else had my attention. A pressure on my mind that came out of nowhere. It wasn't painful, really, just incredibly intense.

It was also simultaneously like nothing I'd ever felt before, and yet also strangely familiar.

"Tabitha?" Steph said, looking down at me in concern. I blinked hard, but the feeling didn't dissipate.

"Something is here," I said to him.

He whispered that same spell again and looked around us with his golden eyes. But when he looked back to me, he said, "I don't sense anything. Are you sure?"

"I'm very sure," I said. "I feel kind of sick to my stomach. And I don't think it's from all the stairs."

"Right," Steph said, and grabbed my arm to pull me to my feet.

"Where are we going?" I asked, trying not to panic as we half-jogged away from the bus stop. Away from our path home.

"A little more out of sight," he said as we headed back to Antonio's apartment building. My heart sank as we pushed our way once more into the bottom of the stairwell, but to my relief, Steph stopped there and pulled out his wand.

"This is going to get a little hairy," he warned me.

"What?" I asked.

"I have to get us home the hard way. I need you to focus on home. Focus with all your will."

I didn't like the firm line his mouth was making. It reminded me of movies where someone was about to pull an arrow out of someone else's shoulder.

One of us was about to get hurt. I just didn't know which one.

"Should I take this off?" I asked, holding up my silver bracelet.

A look of real terror flashed over Steph's face, gone as soon as it manifested. But I knew what I had seen.

"No. No, just focus," he said, and grabbed my hand to squeeze it tight.

As nice as it was to hold hands, I knew he was really just stopping me from taking that bracelet off of my own accord.

Just how hairy was this spell going to be?

Then that pressure on the back of my mind increased tenfold out of nowhere, and I gasped out loud. It still wasn't exactly painful. But it was extremely intrusive.

And maddeningly familiar. Where had I *ever* felt something like this before?

And why couldn't I remember it?

"Focus!" Steph said one last time as he raised his wand to start his spell.

And I pictured the Weal & Woe Bookshop. Not just the sight of the shelves that went on forever under the ever-present soft, glowing, magical lights. But the way that space muffled all sounds under a cozy blanket of silence. The smell of the paper and the ink, the vellum and leather book covers, the dust and occasional musty scent of damp pages.

The crackle of rice paper when someone turned the pages. The crack when the glue in old spines finally broke away in a rain of dried out flakes.

And the warmth of Houdini curled up on my lap as we read together in the window seat of my little nook.

But it was hard to hold on to all of that when the two of us discorporated into ghosts that were then forced through a keyhole, a keyhole of infinite length. We stretched out thinner and thinner, never leaving that stairwell in Geneva even as we reached out for Minneapolis, so very far away.

Like pizza dough. Like taffy. Like fresh noodles. We were forced into stretching, but we could only stretch so far.

And it felt like we were both about to snap.

CHAPTER

TWENTY

For an eternity, it felt like we'd be trapped like that forever. Just stretching out, reaching for something we'd never actually touch.

Then, in a single flash of light, we were both standing in my nook in the Weal & Woe Bookshop, the morning light bathing over us.

I had never been so happy to smell myself surrounded by books in my life. And considering how strongly I feel about those scents, that's really saying something.

But the happiness bubbling inside me dissipated as Steph went from standing beside me to lying facedown at my feet. I tried to catch him, but it happened too fast for me to do more than jam up my fingers trying to grasp his arm.

He fell with a thud. And then he didn't move.

"Steph?" I said, falling to my own knees beside him.

"'Mmm okay," he mumbled into the floor. Which was pretty far from convincing.

"I'll call for the Wizard," I said, hoping that summoning him was the same as summoning Steph. Although if it meant I had to know his actual name, I was going to be out of luck.

"No!" Steph said, flopping out a hand that didn't quite manage to find me. "No, let him rest. Please."

"I'm calling Audrey, then," I said, although in fact I sent her a text. But since all the text said was, "911," it felt more like a call. A call for help.

"Have her bring tea," Steph said. He was still facedown on the carpet, but he was enunciating more clearly now than before.

"What kind of tea?" I asked as I typed the message on my phone.

"Tell her what happened. She'll know what to bring," he said.

That took a lot more typing than I normally like to do on such a tiny keyboard. There were more than a few typos, to be sure, but I hoped she got the gist of it. Then I tucked my phone away and slid an arm under Steph to roll him over then sit him up. He helped, a little, but his final position slumped on the floor with his back against the window seat wasn't exactly filling my heart with confidence.

"What happened?" I asked.

"Exactly what was supposed to happen," he said. But the words came slowly, as if he were infinitely tired, and his eyes weren't quite staying open. "We got home."

"You knew it was going to be like that?" I asked.

"There's a reason we use portals, you know," he said. I could tell by the quirk at the corner of his mouth that he meant that to be joking. But he was going to have to work on his delivery. When he sounded like he was about to die from exhaustion, it didn't really sell the humor.

"Did you feel what I felt?" I asked. "Not the stretching thing. I mean before. That mind pressure thing."

"I don't know anything about that," he said, but opened one eye almost all the way to fix a gaze on me. "You didn't look good when it was happening. I assume it was bad."

"It was... startling, I guess I'd say."

"I didn't detect any magic around us at the time," he said. "No objects or wards or active spells. Not even the remains of spells long gone. Certainly no witches."

"But?" I said. Because I sensed he was holding something back.

"A wizard could hide from that spell," he admitted. "A very powerful wizard."

"Or more than one, for all we know," I said. "I'm glad I panicked, then. It sounds like that was the wise thing to do."

Steph had his eyes closed and didn't attempt to talk. But he did reach out a hand to find mine and just hold it tightly.

We were still sitting like that—shoulder to shoulder, one of us a little more slumped like a sack of potatoes than the other—when I heard the sound of Audrey letting herself in the bookshop door. Not that she had a key. But she didn't need one anymore than I did.

The bookshop knew who we were.

"We're upstairs!" I called. Steph flinched a little at my shouting, but didn't let go of my hand.

I heard her footsteps jogging up the stairs as well as the soft rattle of a china teapot lid that was really meant to be carried far more carefully. But given I had broken all of Audrey's china twice now, and it had been repaired without a sign of damage each time, I wasn't too worried about it.

"You're lucky I've been going through all of Agatha's journals during the slow spells in the teashop, or I would've had no idea what to bring," Audrey was saying as she went from staircase to bookshop aisle. Then she drew up short just as she stepped into the nook itself and saw the two of us sitting on the floor. I watched all the color drain from her face. But she quickly recovered, rushing forward to put the tea tray on the table.

I was wrong about the teapot. What Audrey had brought on the tray was a single tall mug of tea, the kind with its own infuser basket and a lid to hold the steam and the warmth inside. I had seen Agatha use something similar when trying to prepare a medicinal tea for a pushy customer who quickly regretted strong-arming her into just giving it a try.

Having once tasted tea that Agatha had brewed that was

supposed to taste *good*, I shuddered to think what her medicinal tea had tasted like. Like, literally shuddered.

"I only brought the one," Audrey said as she lifted the lid from the mug and sniffed at the emerging steam before putting the lid back on. "And it needs another few minutes, anyway. I'm going to have Liam close up the shop and bring up another. Lucky thing I was in a hurry and left all the ingredients out."

"One should do it, shouldn't it?" I asked, even as I pulled my phone out to check the time. "Your lunch rush is going to be starting soon. You can't just close."

"You're closed," Audrey pointed out as she typed on her phone. When she was finished, she put it away and gave me a stern look. "From your text, I assumed that Steph was the only one trying to teleport himself around the world without a magical focus. You never said you went with him."

"I'm fine," I said. Not that I felt like trying to stand up to prove it. But I was pretty sure that was just because of all the stairs.

I was prepared to blame everything on staircases. There were simply too many of them.

"You're probably not fine," Steph mumbled to me. His hand in mine was still grasping me strongly, but he wasn't quite opening his eyes even as he turned his face towards me.

"Neither of you are fine," Audrey said, and lifted the lid from the mug again. This time the smell of the steam seemed to satisfy her, and she carefully lifted the infuser basket out and tipped it to let as much liquid as possible drip out of it. Then she squatted down in front of Steph. "Take it," she ordered him.

He had to take his hand away from mine, as he needed both to hold the mug steady. But he perked up a little just from the smell, something sort of minty but a lot more like eucalyptus. He took a sip and made a face, but took a second sip before Audrey could send more than a look of annoyance his way.

"We were looking for Antonio," I said. "We didn't find him. Or the book. Although I think we just let someone potentially dangerous know we were looking for him and it. Which might be bad."

"You're not going back to Geneva," Steph put in between sips of tea.

"You're not either, then," I said.

"Unless the Wizard sends me," Steph said.

I decided not to argue with that. I doubted I would win, anyway. But more than that, I doubted the Wizard would send him there alone. Not after I told him what I had sensed there.

Or thought I had sensed. My memory of it was already fading.

I started to try to get to my feet, but before I had managed a single feeble attempt, Audrey's hands on my shoulders pinned me down.

"Just sit still. Liam will be here with your tea in a minute," she said.

"I need a notebook. A journal or something," I said.

"Isn't that it right beside you?" Audrey said with a frown.

I looked down and saw a leather-bound journal on the floor by my left hand. It looked like it had just tumbled to the floor from the window seat behind me. Only I didn't have a journal besides my dream journal, and that one was still up in my bedroom.

"Thank you, bookshop," I murmured as I pulled the journal onto my knees and groped around until I found a pen that had somehow fallen between my butt and the wall.

I was still writing down every detail I could remember as quickly as I could, all too aware of how those details were slipping away even as I tried to pin them down, when a steaming mug of eucalyptus-smelling tea was suddenly between me and the page.

"Drink this," Audrey commanded.

"Drink it," Steph backed her up. His voice was sounding stronger, and when I glanced over at him, it was to see him looking at me with both eyes opened. They were still bloodshot from his sleepless night, but they were open.

"I'm not sure I'm going to remember anything more, anyway," I said as I set the journal aside and took the mug of tea.

As much as it had smelled of mint, the taste was bitter, the kind of bitter that sucks all the moisture out of your tongue just tasting it.

"Honey?" I asked.

"Not with this, sorry," Audrey said.

She didn't sound sorry at all.

"Why were you in Geneva if Antonio is in Canada?" Liam asked. He was standing just behind Audrey but mimicking her "I'm not angry, just disappointed" posture, looming over Steph and me with his arms crossed.

"We didn't know he was in Canada until we were just about to leave," I said.

"A lot came up right after breakfast," Liam said. "Barnardo came running back down to tell us, but when we came here looking for you, we saw the shop was closed."

"Barnardo found out about Canada?" I asked. But that didn't make any sense.

And Liam was already shaking his head. "No, that was prosaic sources. My newsfeeds."

"When we saw you were out, I went ahead and put Barnardo on the Canada trail," Audrey said. "Antonio was spotted on prosaic cameras there, but Barnardo's whisper network extends to Toronto and Quebec. He'll let us know if he hears anything."

"I kind of doubt Antonio is going to seek refuge in a magical community after living outside of it for so long, but I guess anything is possible," I said. "I just wish we knew if he even had the book. I'd hate to chase him down only to find he never even had it."

"We kind of thought the same, but there's more," Liam said.

"Cleopatra Manx's brother Octavio is missing," Audrey said.

"What does that have to do with—" I started, but then interrupted myself with a slap to my forehead. "No. Right. Blackmail?"

"That's the assumption," Audrey said. "Needless to say, Barnardo was beyond delighted at the prospect that the Manx family was about to have a public societal disaster on their hands."

"And yet you convinced him to go to Canada?" I said. And despite it all, I could feel a grin bursting out of me.

"My Audrey is a master at persuasion," Liam said.

"Barnardo's not exactly objective enough to be our source on Manx family info," Audrey said reasonably, even as her cheeks burst into flames.

"In all likelihood, Octavio Manx isn't even missing," Steph said. "He's just lying low until the rumors blow over. And, honestly, it wouldn't be the first time. The man attracts salacious controversy."

"If half of what Barnardo had to say about him was true, it only makes sense," Liam said. "His sort of behavior is bound to attract commentary."

Clearly, there was a lot I didn't know about the reputations of the various members of the Manx family. They were the closest thing the witches in America had to royalty, and that tended to attract a lot of attention. But it wasn't the sort of thing I'd ever been drawn to myself. But a lot of other students in the academies followed the stories of the Manx family's lives with slavish devotion. And not much care about separating fact from fiction.

But the name Octavio wasn't ringing any specific bells for me. I was just about to ask for more details when I heard the sound of the bell over the door downstairs chiming. The one that leads out into the prosaic world.

"Did you leave that open?" I asked Audrey and Liam.

"No. The sign still says *Closed*," Audrey said with a frown.

"I made sure the door was locked after I came in," Liam said. "Or, at least, I thought I did."

"I'll go chase whoever it is away," Audrey said, but took one last moment to point at the mug in my hands. "Finish that before it gets cold."

I made a face, but swallowed down the last of the contents. A lot of sediment had collected at the bottom, and the whole thing would've been better when it was tongue-searingly hot.

We all heard a male voice speaking to Audrey, although the words themselves were swallowed up by the rows of bookshelves and staircases between the two of them and us.

Then we heard two sets of footsteps coming up the stairs.

"Who would come in through the prosaic door?" Steph asked me, even as he struggled to his feet. I tried to get up as well, but my knees were still all jelly. I made it as far as the window seat before deciding that sitting on that was at least an improvement over sitting on the floor.

"Tabitha?" Audrey called as she came down the aisle towards the nook. I hadn't heard her sound so hesitant and unsure of herself since the day I met her, and I was immediately on edge.

Then she appeared, but my gaze jumped right past her even before she stepped aside to let the man behind her stride into the open space of my nook.

I couldn't look away. Because as much as the young man standing there was a stranger to me, I knew I should know him. Everything about him, from his ice-blue eyes to his long, silken, raven-colored hair, was so familiar.

I had no idea who he was.

Only that he looked more like my mother than I did.

CHAPTER

TWENTY-ONE

His first words were, "Well, this is a bit awkward."

And I instantly had to fight back a wave of hysterical laughter. Which made me choke. Audrey rushed forward to take the tea mug from my hands and set it safely back on its tray.

The young man just stood there looking confused, like he wasn't sure if he should be concerned or offended by my behavior.

"The bookshop let you in," Steph said. His complexion was still pale from our return trip from Geneva, and his eyes were still red at the edges from his lack of sleep, but he was standing in his most imposing posture. And he was using his apprentice voice. The one that heavily implied that he spoke with the authority of the Wizard. It had been so long since I'd heard him speak that way, I had forgotten how it sent chills down my spine.

And not in a good way. Although at the moment, it was the stranger taking the brunt of it. And I could tell he was fighting the urge to squirm.

"Of course it did," the stranger said, making a decent show of pretending not to be intimidated by Steph. "It's my uncle's shop."

177

Then he stepped forward, offering Steph his hand. "Introductions are probably in order here. I am Mercutio Ward, nephew to Carlo Greene-Baxter, and brother to Tabitha... I understand you go by Greene?"

That last was directed at me, and now everyone was looking at me at once. It was a lot.

I swallowed and said, more softly than I had intended, "It's all I've ever known to go by."

"Really? Mother never told you anything about the Ward family?" He sounded surprised by that, but not in an aggressive way.

To my amazement, it was Audrey who spoke next. "The Ward family? From Chicago?"

"Oh, you've heard of us?" Mercutio said, and gave her a smile that was clearly meant to be disarming. It looked practiced. Like he deployed it a lot.

I bet it usually worked, too.

But Audrey, as much as her cheeks pinkened ever so slightly, sounded not at all impressed when she said, "We've been investigating the robbery of the Talbot Book Repository. You know, chasing down some leads about potential blackmail victims. People who might have had a motive to kill a bookseller, rob his safe, and burn his shop to the ground."

But Mercutio didn't register any shock at this accusation. If anything, he just seemed amused. "Yes, I'm afraid my father and one of his cousins would definitely be on the list of suspects. If such blackmail even existed. Which, there is no proof it did. And there's definitely no proof it does now."

"Convenient," Liam mumbled, mostly to himself. But Mercutio just shrugged.

"Why have we never met?" I asked him. "I mean, you seem to know all about my uncle and my mother. And me."

"That's a long story, sister," he said.

"All right, then," I said, and lifted my chin. "I'll settle for why you're here now."

"Oh. I thought that was obvious," he said. He looked from me to Audrey and Liam and then to Steph.

"It's been a long day," I said, ignoring the fact that it wasn't quite lunchtime.

"You want me to spell it out?" he asked.

"Yes," I said.

"In front of everyone?" he asked. He took a step closer to me, like we were somehow going to have a private conversation when the three other people in the room were well within the reach of whispers.

"These are my friends. Audrey Mirken, Stephanos Underwood, and Liam Kelly. I trust all of them with my life," I said.

Mercutio took another step closer, speaking almost in my ear. "Far be it from me to tell you your business, sister, but that one there is a prosaic."

"Oh, I know," I said. "He's part of the team. Say your piece or go, I don't care which."

Which was the farthest thing from true. I was pretty sure if he turned to go, I would throw myself at his feet and wrap my arms around his legs to keep him from leaving before telling me everything he knew.

But at the same time, there was something about him that was rubbing me the wrong way. Maybe it was how he kept dropping nuggets of information, implying he knew everything about me when I hadn't even known he existed two minutes before.

Or maybe it was just that he looked so much like my mother. And I had learned to be cautious with how much I trusted her.

Mostly, I was feeling more drawn out now than before I had drunk Audrey's restorative tea. Which was probably a good thing, knowing how much I was not in top form at this moment. I wasn't in the sort of head space I wanted to be in before making major life decisions.

Like whether or not I should trust a man who showed up out of nowhere claiming to be my brother.

Not that any part of me doubted that was true. I knew it was true just by looking at him. I could feel it in my blood and in my bones. This man was my brother.

What I didn't know was whether that meant I could trust him. Maybe he was my evil twin.

Mercutio licked his bottom lip as he considered what to do. That, too, looked like a practiced gesture. Everything about him felt like a performance, really. Like I was watching a piece of Japanese theater. I knew it was artifice, but I wasn't familiar enough with the culture and the form to decode it all.

But in the end, he simply said, "Very well." Then he gestured for all of us to join him around the table.

My table.

I wasn't the only one feeling proprietary about it, however, as when Mercutio attempted to take the chair at what would be the head of the table, Liam stopped him by simply saying, "That's Houdini's chair."

"Of course," Mercutio said with a bow of his head, and slid one chair over.

Not giving any hint as to whether the name Houdini meant anything to him or not.

Mercutio waited for us all to settle into chairs with his hands folded in front of him. Then he sat back in his chair in so relaxed a pose I half-expected him to throw a leg over the arm of the chair like a jester sitting on the king's throne.

"First of all, it's not about the blackmail," Mercutio said. "That's a... how do the prosaics say it?" he asked, turning to Liam.

Liam swallowed. Only someone who had known him as long as Audrey and I had would recognize that as a supreme show of irritation in him. But his voice was level as he said, "A red herring."

"Right! It's a red herring," Mercutio said. He brushed at an invisible bit of nothing on the knee of his dark navy pants. "It's about the book. You know which one I mean, sister. It's always been about the book."

I chewed at my lip, deliberating. It was possible he *did* know all about the book. But it was also possible that he was just using bits of things he knew to fish for more details. It was the same sense I got from him every time he mentioned my family or called me his sister. It didn't quite feel... solid.

Steph glanced at me, then fixed his gaze on Mercutio. "The book Prospero was meant to deliver to us was likely not of any interest to anybody. It was merely a scientific text, and an obscure one from a lesser mathematician at that."

"Steph. Come on," Mercutio said with a grin. "We both know that's not the whole story."

"Do you have the book?" I asked him. Because why else would he be here?

He turned to me with a warm smile, and I felt something inside myself loosen a little. That smile broke the sense that he was a younger, male version of my mother. My mother never smiled like that. She never showed that many teeth or scrunched so much around the eyes.

Then I realized what that smile really reminded me of, and I bit down on a gasp before it could escape me.

It was my own smile. The one I used to get teased about back in my schooldays. Because my cheeks would puff up like I was a squirrel storing nuts for winter.

Only on Mercutio, it was less reminiscent of a squirrel and more just friendly and charismatic.

I should practice in a mirror. See if I could bring my own overly enthusiastic grin back down to his more effective level.

"I promise you, if there's anyone in this universe that wants a look at that book as much as you do, it's me," he said. And I believed him. But then he unhooked his leg from the arm of the chair to sit back with a shrug. "But I don't have it."

"Then why are you here?" Steph asked. "The timing is... suspect."

He cast the briefest of glances at me when he said that. I'm not sure anyone else even saw him do it. But it was enough for me to realize just what had him worried.

The Tower. It was recovering, but still not operating at full strength.

And it was part of the Square. The Wizard protected the Square, even more than the elaborate wards did. But he was recovering, too.

But wasn't all that mostly about threats of discovery from the prosaic world?

I really wished I could grab Steph by the arm and drag him somewhere private to talk all that through. But my brother was watching me so closely I didn't even dare stop focusing on my poker face, let alone try to casually step away.

"But surely you've heard the news?" Mercutio said, looking from one to the next of us.

"Are we talking about Canada?" Audrey asked carefully.

"Canada? No, that's another red herring," Mercutio said with a dismissive wave. "No, Antonio Talbot was never really in Canada."

"So he *is* getting magical help," I said.

"Of course he is. He's being chased by some of the most powerful wizards in the world," Mercutio said. "Believe me, he wants to get that book to you first. And *that's* why I'm here now." He shot Steph a triumphant look, but Steph just ignored him, lost in his own thoughts.

"Because you know where he is?" I asked.

"I do," Mercutio said. "Because I helped him get here. To Minneapolis, not the Square," he hastened to add. "He's still very distrustful of magical communities, but I'm sure you can understand why."

"Why?" Liam asked. But Mercutio acted like he hadn't heard that word.

"Let me get this straight," Steph said, the edge to his voice less authoritative and more dangerous now. "You turn up just when Tabitha needs you, offering just what she needs, and we're supposed to trust you to take her right to it? Because only you know the way?"

Mercutio actually looked offended by that. "Of course not!" he said. "Any of you or all of you can come. It's not a problem."

He shot a single glance Liam's way, one I barely caught. Clearly, he had some cutting remark ready about his estimation of Liam's value, but at the last second left it unexpressed.

It was scarcely odd for a member of the magical community to have such opinions of prosaic people. It was all too common, in fact.

But it kind of bugged me to realize it was in my family.

He did know that our uncle had married a prosaic, didn't he?

"There is a time issue," Mercutio said, tapping a fingertip on the tabletop as if pointing to something on an invisible agenda. "We really do have to go pretty much now. But I couldn't help noticing that your shop was closed anyway, so it doesn't seem like it would be inconvenient for you. So what do you say?"

I looked over at Steph, and he looked back at me. If I looked half as exhausted as he did, I was glad I couldn't see it.

But I was pretty sure the resolve in his eyes matched my own, too. And that resolve won out over exhaustion.

"Fine," I said out loud to my brother, even as my eyes stayed locked on Steph's. "We'll go. Now, if we must."

"Excellent," Mercutio said, slapping his hands loudly and then rubbing them together. "We'll get this book, no problem, and then we'll have all the time in the world for catching up." Then he leaned forward, waiting until I met his blue eyes before saying, "I'm so glad I finally found you, sister. That I can be of service to you straight away is just icing on the cake."

I didn't know what to say to that, so I opted for just a single nod.

But I really hoped he was right about having all the time in the world for catching up after. Because all of this was happening too fast for me. I preferred my life at "whiling away time in a bookshop" speed.

And this? Was the opposite of that.

TWENTY-TWO

After a brief discussion, it was decided that Liam and Audrey would go back to the teashop to open for business and try to track down Barnardo if they could, ideally before he actually left for Canada.

Steph and I would go with Mercutio, although exactly where we were going, he wouldn't say.

"Can I go talk to Houdini before I go?" I asked. "I don't want him to worry if he finds me gone."

"We really don't have time," Mercutio started to say, but Steph cut him off.

"The Wizard will let him know," he said. He was speaking casually, only looking at me and even then not particularly intently. But I got his hidden message.

The Wizard knew where we were, and would continue to know where we were. I wasn't sure if this was something he always knew about his apprentice, or something the two of them had cooked up just since Steph had started going out into the world with me. But the latter made a certain kind of sense.

Clearly, I attracted danger wherever I went.

"Be safe," Audrey said, giving me a hug before we parted ways at the main floor of the bookshop. She and Liam were heading out the prosaic door, and I had a strong urge to be very sure it was secured behind them before I also left the shop.

"I will. And I'll have my phone, assuming it works wherever we're going." I shot Mercutio a pointed look, but he offered no more information than he had before.

Liam looked like he wanted to say something to me, but after a glance over at my brother, standing too close behind us, he just shook his head and let it go.

"I'll work on the spell when we get back, I promise," I said. Although I was pretty sure that wasn't what he had been about to ask about.

Liam chuckled softly. "Tabitha, if you find what you're looking for, I know what I want will come second. And that's fine. I'm perfectly capable of finding work the old-fashioned way."

"Thanks for understanding," I said.

Then he and Audrey were gone, out into the hot August midday. I shut the door before the blast of humidity could start me sweating too much.

For all the good it did me. Two minutes later, Steph, Mercutio and I went out the back door into the open courtyard of the Square, and there was nothing to stop me from sweating after that point. Especially as where Mercutio led us was into the hedge maze.

At first, I assumed he was leading us to the portal at the heart of the maze. That made the most sense; it was the most traveled path through the maze, easy to follow, and an understandable destination given that the portal could take at least Steph anywhere he chose. I would have trouble without Steph's help, not having access to that sort of disciplined magic.

But I wasn't sure about Mercutio. If what Steph and I had theorized was true—and it certainly felt like it had to be, now that I had discovered I did, indeed, have a twin—that would make Mercutio proficient in the magic of order. That sounded like something perfectly suited to using the portal to travel along established magical pathways.

Only, he had come into the bookshop through the prosaic door. Which didn't make any sense if this was his point of entry into the Square.

And then I realized we weren't even on that heavily traveled path through the maze anymore.

But I knew where we were going. Because, as wild and unvisited as this section of the maze appeared with the hedges around us all shaggy and overgrown, I had been here before.

It hadn't ended well.

"Where are we going?" I demanded, and instantly stopped walking. I crossed my arms, prepared to stare down my brother.

"You know where we're going," Mercutio said, gesturing for me to keep walking, to catch up.

But I didn't move. And Steph didn't either. He took a half a step back, as if he didn't want to get caught between us. Then he just waited there, hands in his pockets, not quite looking amused, but not far from it.

"The last time I came down this way, I was being lured into a trap," I said.

"I know," he said. Maddeningly. Because I still couldn't tell if he was lying or if he was telling the truth.

"So you think I'm just going to walk blindly into another one?" I asked.

Mercutio gave a dry, frustrated laugh. He waved a hand in Steph's direction. "If I were luring you into a trap, would I let this guy come along?"

"You might, if you thought you could get the upper-hand," I said.

He chuckled again, shaking his head in a wry manner. But he walked back to a more comfortable talking distance from me. "I know the name Stephanos Underwood. He was a year behind me and in a different academy, but ritual magicians are very competitive. As you, no doubt, know. I have no illusions about being able to get the upper-hand. Not when he's here."

He didn't wait for me to answer, just continued on towards the alcove in the maze where the hidden exit lurked beneath a grate in the ground.

I looked over at Steph. "Did you know my brother too, then?"

"I didn't know he was your brother," Steph said. "But I've heard the name Mercutio Ward before, yes."

"And?" I prompted in a fierce whisper, stepping closer to him. Mercutio was still walking away with his back to us, approaching the next turn that would take him out of our sight.

"Like he said, we went to different academies. I didn't know him personally at all. But by reputation, he was a decent enough ritual magician," Steph said with a shrug. He wasn't bothering to whisper at all, I noticed.

"Decent?" I said.

"He wasn't *stellar*," Steph said. "I mean, he ranked higher than Audrey did. Although she would've been four years behind him, so they were never directly competing. But you get the general idea."

"All I know is that Audrey's class ranking has no bearing on her actual abilities as a witch," I said grumpily. The hot, humid air was stifling inside the confines of the hedge maze, and I was regretting not grabbing a bottle of water before we headed out. Of course, I hadn't realized we were going this way.

But Steph leaned close to whisper in my ear a word barely louder than a breath, "Exactly."

Then he pulled back, his dark brown eyes giving me a significant look, before strolling on after Mercutio, his hands still casually thrust into his pockets.

Of course, it would be the smart play not to underestimate my brother, or any ritual magician, for that matter.

But if Mercutio's ideas of what Steph was capable of were based on what he had seen when they were in their schooldays, when Steph had been far and away at the top of his class and any other, my brother would still be shortchanging what Steph was capable of.

I didn't think he was, though. And I got the sense Steph didn't think he was, either.

I hoped after a good night's sleep and a couple of hearty meals, my brain would be clear enough to know for sure what I thought of my brother. But until then I was caught in this weird mental space, where everything he said sounded completely truthful and sincere, and yet my gut was still screaming not to trust it.

I hoped my gut was just stuck in panic mode. But there was no way to know for sure. Not until it was too late.

By the time I reached our destination, Mercutio already had the grate opened up and had disappeared down into the dark tunnel below. Steph motioned for me to go first, and I slipped my legs down into the shaft, feeling around until I caught one of the iron bars of the ladder. Then I climbed down into the chilly but still humid space below.

"If it's the underground canal system you're looking for, there's a station right under the pub," I said to the spot in the darkness that I was pretty sure was my brother. "We could've saved ourselves some time."

"It will scarcely surprise you to hear that Antonio is a little paranoid about us being followed," he said back, a little further ahead than I had thought. I quickened my steps a little.

"Did he give you any hint as to why he killed his brother?" I asked.

For a moment, I didn't think Mercutio was going to answer at all. Then I found myself colliding into the back of his broad shoulders. We had reached the point where our narrow tunnel of darkness met the magically lit interior of the Minneapolis sewer system that ran around the northeast corner of the Square. He stepped through it, then turned to face me as I came out after him, rubbing my nose a little.

His shoulders were like rocks.

He took my hand to draw me out of Steph's way, or so I thought. But then his gaze caught mine, and I realized he hadn't wanted to answer me in the dark. He wanted to be looking me in the eye when he spoke what came next.

The magical globes of light that lit this stretch of sewer had a greenish-yellow tinge to them. That cast a sickly sort of light on most of our surroundings. But somehow the blue of his eyes picked up only the most emerald tones of the green, turning his eyes into a lovely aquamarine.

It was so unfair. How had he gotten all of our mother's casual, always beautiful genes? And what did our father even look like?

"Tabitha," Mercutio said, dragging my mind back to the task at hand. "Antonio didn't kill Prospero. And he didn't burn down his apartment either, although I know Prospero thought differently."

"Then who did?" I asked.

"If he knows, he won't tell me," he said with a weary sigh. "He is running from them, whoever they are. But he won't speak his suspicions out loud."

"But he trusts you? I mean, he's actually going to meet us, wherever we're going, right?"

"He is very anxious to get rid of the book," he said. "Very anxious. And after I explained why you and I need to have it, he was eager to give it to us."

"I thought he was selling it to us," I said.

"No, that was Prospero's plan," Mercutio said. "If the book had passed down to Antonio, none of this would have ever happened. But Prospero put the word out about what he'd found, and while the Wizard may have thought he'd locked down the chatter... Well, that's all but impossible. Something rare and forbidden like this, people listen for news like that."

Steph had emerged behind us and was looking up and down the water channel that ran at our feet.

"Oh, it's coming," Mercutio told him.

"You have to summon boats to the pub station," Steph said.

"They don't just turn up on a schedule. We're too much of a back-water for constant service."

"I'm sure," Mercutio said, even as I saw the prow of a boat coming around the bed in the sewer behind him. Down this chan-nel, which wasn't even part of the magical underground canal system. It was an abandoned offshoot. Nothing should just *happen* by.

From the way Mercutio was grinning at me, I guessed my thoughts were clear on my face. But he just put out a hand, and the boat drew to a halt beside him.

"Things just have a way of falling into place for me," he said with a shrug. Then he held out a hand to help me step down into the boat.

I ignored his hand to get down on my own, nearly upending the boat in the process. I guess I'd made both my point and his point at once, but he didn't say a word. He just waited for Steph to climb down after me before getting in himself. He sat with his back resting against the prow of the boat. The greenish light from the lantern hanging from the prow behind his head cast his face in eerie shad-ows, but I could still clearly see his eyes. They almost glowed out of the darkness, like a beacon of good will.

"What's our father's name?" I asked.

"Benvolio Ward," Steph said before Mercutio could speak. "He's a very prominent ritual magician. He serves on the local council in Chicago."

"*Did* serve," Mercutio corrected him. "He has recently stepped down to focus on some personal matters."

"He was gunning for the High Council. Aggressively," Steph said.

"Again, he *was*," Mercutio agreed, apparently unbothered by Steph's darkening tone. "But something has come up that changed his plans. Nothing to do with the two of us, sister. No worries there."

"It must've been very recently," Steph said coolly.

"Yesterday," Mercutio said. It was hard to tell with his face in those shadows, but I thought he might be smirking just a little.

I swallowed hard before asking the real question that plagued my mind. "Does he know all about me, like you do? I mean, where I am and everything I've been doing?"

My heart was beating right in the center of my throat, kind of choking me, as I waited for his answer.

But when it came, it was probably the last thing I expected for him to say.

"You know, I've never met him? Not that I can recall. I have no idea what he knows or doesn't know about either of us." And his shadowy form shrugged.

"But you have his name," I said.

"Apparently, the Ward family insisted," he said with a dismissive wave. "Not that they've ever had anything to do with me, either."

That thing before, the thing I thought was the last thing I ever expected him to say? Wasn't.

No, that would be the *next* thing he said to me. Still oh so casually, but I could feel the intensity of those eyes kicking up a notch. Eagerly watching for my reaction as he said, "No, I'm afraid it's just been me and Mother, on our own together since the day he took you away."

TWENTY-THREE

Mercutio refused to explain anything further, insisting we had to focus only on the task at hand.

It made for a long, uncomfortably quiet boat ride through the dark sewers that crossed in and out of the prosaic world.

I admit it. I was sulking. But I was annoyed.

I don't know how many quays are connected by the magical underground canal system under Minneapolis. I had only ever been to three: the one under the pub in the Square, the one under the Foshay Tower in modern Minneapolis, and the one that connects to the mirror image vestige of the former Metropolitan Building that is hidden, upside-down, under the lot in Minneapolis where it had once existed on the surface.

The quay our boat bumped to a halt against was, not surprisingly, not one I'd been to before. I knew we were under Minneapolis proper, not the former city of St. Anthony where the Square was located, because we had gone through the channel that passed under the Mississippi River. It was hard to miss that; from the magical world underground, the Saint Anthony Falls were still as magnificent as they'd been before the disastrous collapse of the Eastman Tunnel in 1869.

Witches are very sentimental, even about prosaic things. Perhaps especially about prosaic things. I mean, keeping a reflection of a massive waterfall alive, if hidden to the modern world, was one thing. But setting up your local government in a preserved if inverted actual prosaic-built edifice? Which was what the Metropolitan Building was today? That's pretty much the definition of sentimental.

But when I had climbed out of the boat onto the stone quay Mercutio had taken us to, I knew we were in no such heavily populated place. The quay was lit by globes of greenish magical light, and the turnstile looked clean and well-maintained. But the dried remains of whatever detritus the last heavy rainfall had swept over the stones under my feet had lain undisturbed for some time before my sneakered feet had stirred it up.

"Where are we?" I asked, trying to peek up through the holes in the sewer covers overhead. I could see the bottoms of passing cars, a lot of traffic, even for this hour in the afternoon. But I was nowhere near familiar enough with Minneapolis to guess just where we were.

"The planetarium project," Steph said before Mercutio could answer. Probably with something vague.

But it wasn't like I understood Steph's answer any better.

"The what, now?" I asked.

"A place even more abandoned than that tunnel under the Square," Mercutio said, waving for us to follow him down what, to my eyes, was a particularly dark tunnel.

"When the prosaics remodeled the public library over our heads, they closed down the planetarium that had been there for years," Steph explained as we walked into that darkness. It was only a semi-darkness. I could see well enough to know where the walls were on either side of us. And that they were covered with an ooze better not brushed against.

Especially not now that I was wearing my new clothes.

"That's a shame," I said.

"There is a museum that's part of the local university that has a planetarium now," Steph said. "But there was a gap of a few years between the two. Some of the local witches got a little nostalgic and attempted to bring down the remains of the old planetarium to preserve it down below. You know, like we do."

"That feels like something Minnesota witches do more than other witches," I said.

"Yeah, I've noticed that too," Steph said. "Anyway, they didn't have enough support to get much without the prosaics noticing. So there's an open space, and some magical astrolabes are stored there, but the only thing they took from above is the seating."

"That's kind of sad," I said.

"It's also as remote as you can get inside the magical network under this city," Mercutio said from ahead of us. "Which is why Antonio is hiding out here."

I heard the change in volume of his voice as he disappeared from the tunnel ahead of us, moving into a larger, more echoing space.

I didn't have the faintest sense of danger around us, but it was still a comfort when Steph slid his hand into mine as we turned the same corner into that larger space.

Even as I knew it was his left hand in mine, because his right hand was already brandishing his wand. Just in case.

"Antonio?" Mercutio was calling into the darkness in the corners of the room around us. I heard Steph mumble a few words, then lift his wand to shoot out a silver moon the size of a beach ball. It zipped to the center of the room to float near the roof, casting a light that wasn't too terribly bright, but which penetrated everywhere.

"No lights! No lights!" a voice hissed.

"We aren't conducting business in the dark," Steph said, even as I struggled to pinpoint where that voice had come from. "I serve the Wizard," he went on, and as always, the capital letter was apparent just in his tone. It was scarcely surprising that no one ever asked which wizard he meant.

"I'm sure you think that should put me at ease," the man said, "But honestly, I've known too many wizards."

I finally caught sight of him. He was standing behind a stack of planetarium seats, some reclined and some upright. As different as he had looked from his brother in the photograph from their school-days, he looked far more like his brother now than like the older version of himself that I would have expected.

Perhaps it was the hair. They shared the unwashed, untamed look.

Or perhaps it was the sense that they had both recently escaped a fire of some kind. Prospero may have been dressed in the old school trousers and waistcoat look many magical types favored, while his brother seemed to be wearing an athletic sweatshirt for some sports team I couldn't identify over a very worn pair of jeans. But just as Prospero's sleeves had been crumbling into ash when I had seen him, Antonio's sweatshirt cuffs were blackened and breaking away.

As if the sight of his clothes were some sort of trigger, the usual sewer smells that pervaded the magical underground canal system faded away. All I could smell was burning books.

But this burn smell had a particular signature I recognized at once.

He smelled like the remains of the Talbot Book Repository.

"You were there," I said to him, and he jumped and twitched as if he hadn't seen me standing there, almost directly under the glowing moon. "You were at the Talbot Book Repository when it burned down."

"Well, of course I was there!" Antonio snapped. "How else could I have gotten this?" And he gripped the book in his arms more tightly to his chest.

"You said he didn't do it," I said to Mercutio.

"He didn't," Mercutio said with infinite patience, even as Antonio shouted, "I didn't! I never!"

"Tabitha," Steph said to me, softly. Then he rolled his eyes towards Antonio, begging me to notice something.

To notice the orange glow to Antonio's right hand. It was a dark orange, and dim. But it was growing brighter and lighter by degrees.

"I'm sorry. I jumped to conclusions," I said, raising both my hands for good measure so he could see I meant no harm.

"I would never hurt my brother! He would still be alive if he had just listened to me!" Antonio said, the last words ending in a shriek of sorrow.

"Prospero was already dead when Antonio got there to warn him," Mercutio said, although for whose benefit, I wasn't sure. He was giving me information, but he seemed more intent on calming Antonio down.

Not that I could blame him for wanting to do that.

"He was?" I said, pitching my voice to the politest of inquiries as I looked to Antonio. I was tempted to try batting my eyes at him innocently, but that felt like overplaying it.

"He told me he was going to burn all the blackmail material, but with no witnesses to say it was truly done, who would ever believe it?" Antonio said. His hand had brightened to a dark yellow, but it seemed to be paused at that hue. For the moment.

"It was a cursed inheritance for both of you, I'm sure," I said.

"They promised they would close all accounts before they died," Antonio said, and wiped viciously at his nose with the sleeve of his right arm. "They swore everyone they were blackmailing would know the family was out of the business before it passed on to us. But I never believed them. I never did."

"No, of course not. In fact, you left our world because of it, didn't you?" I asked.

"Not just that," he said. "But that would've been reason enough. But not for Prospero. He always believed everything they said, even though he knew they were doing terrible things. And that it would destroy us all in the end. As it has."

"You didn't ask for this," Steph said. "But that doesn't change the fact that you are in real danger now. I know the Manx family and the

Ward family for certain are looking for you. I presume there are others."

"Dozens," Antonio said, looking around as if some of them might be standing behind him even now. Then he swung around to point that glowing hand at Steph. "Including your so-called master, the Wizard."

"The Wizard has no fear of blackmail," Steph said. "But he is exactly the one to help you now. He can bear witness to what you've said, that all the blackmail materials were destroyed in that fire. The fire that your brother set, isn't that so?"

"I don't know," Antonio said, almost aggressively. "The whole shop was on fire when I got there. And he was already dead on the floor. All that remained in the safe was this accursed book. So I took it and ran. It's all I have to negotiate with."

"It has value to us, no question about that. But it's not why we're going to help you. And we *are* going to help you, Antonio," Steph said.

Antonio said nothing, but his eyes narrowed suspiciously. And his glowing hand moved closer to the book.

"The Wizard already knows the blackmail material was consumed in the fire," I said, which was a total guess, but Steph confirmed my words with a quick nod. "He hasn't told the High Council, because why would he? It's not their business. But if you can tell him the names of all the families looking for you, he can contact them himself. As a fellow victim, and being that he's the Wizard, they'll believe him. You'll be safe."

"Safe," Antonio said, as if the word tasted bitter on his tongue. "What good does that even do me, being safe? I don't even know why I'm still here. Why did I bring this book here?"

"I asked you to," Mercutio said. "Don't you remember?"

"Do I remember?" Antonio asked.

I suddenly wished I had asked Liam more questions about Antonio's history of mental illness. Like just what he had been diagnosed with, what the symptoms were, how bad they were.

Whether he was off his medication since he'd been on the run, and what that might mean?

But looking at him now as he rubbed at his forehead with the heel of his glowing hand, I didn't feel like he was any danger to anyone, not even himself. He just radiated a weary melancholy. More melancholy than any one person should try to carry.

"Antonio," I said.

And then I made a mistake. I took a step towards him.

He stepped back, three steps in stumbling succession, until his back was pressed against the glistening stone of the wall behind him.

"Maybe it wasn't about the blackmail after all," Antonio said, looking down at the book in his arms. "Maybe that was a lie."

"No, Antonio. We've been over this," Mercutio said, waving for me to stand still even though I had already stopped moving. "I can protect you from them for a time. The Wizard can protect you longer. And we will. We just need that book."

"But not until you're ready to give it up!" I said. Because Antonio was clutching that book so tightly to his chest, it was like a security blanket in the grip of a very nervous, about to explode toddler. "You hold on to it until you're ready to give it up. Okay? Antonio? Okay?"

Antonio snuffled, then wiped his sleeve across his nose again. He looked like he was pulling himself together. He really did.

But then he looked at each of us in turn. First Steph, then me, and lastly Mercutio.

And then the glow in his hand cranked up with startling speed.

"No!" I cried, and started to rush forward, but both Steph and Mercutio reached out to stop me.

"I'm so sorry," Antonio said. But he didn't look apologetic so much as terrified. And I didn't think he was apologizing to us.

With a crackling roar, the light in his hand became a beacon of flame that consumed first the book and then his clothes, and then the man himself.

The heat was intense, like it was burning away my eyebrows in the brief second before I turned my face away and stumbled to the far side of the room and its suddenly welcome damp cold.

"Why?" I asked, over and over again.

But neither Steph nor Mercutio had an answer for me.

When the fire burned itself out, there was nothing left but a pile of ash.

Mercutio started ranting in some language I didn't know. It was noteworthy both that it was a language I couldn't even guess at—I didn't think any of those still existed—and that even without knowing what he was saying, I was certain he was cursing. When even that didn't burn off enough of his excess emotion, he started pacing the far corner of the room.

Maybe he was more like me than I thought. I mean, my uncle Carlo also did order magic, and I couldn't ever imagine him reacting like that. It felt like chaos energy to me.

But I was too emotionally wrung out to say anything about it. Surely there'd be time later for parsing out who we each were, and what that all would mean.

Instead, I watched, hugging myself tightly, as Steph picked his way around the unscorched planetarium seating and dug through the pile of still smoking ash. I thought at first he was trying to somehow find a way to separate human remains from book remains.

But when he came back to me, he had something in his hand. Something that flashed gold in the light from the moon globe before he tucked it away in his pocket.

"Come on," he said, putting an arm around my shoulders. "There's nothing more to do here. We might as well go home."

I nodded silently.

But then my brother said, brightly, "Right. Home." I was just wondering what that word meant to him when he said, "To the Square."

Then he led the way back to the quay and the waiting boat.

CHAPTER

TWENTY-FOUR

We took the boat to the exact same location in the abandoned tunnel of the magical underground canal system, the one right in front of the hidden tunnel to the heart of the hedge maze.

But when Steph and I had climbed out of the boat, we found ourselves completely alone. There was no sign of Mercutio.

There wasn't even any sign of the boat we'd taken to get there.

"What does *that* mean?" I all but wailed. I was, to put it mildly, feeling pretty exasperated.

"It's probably not safe to discuss it here," Steph said, even as he hustled me into the dark tunnel. "In fact, even the bookshop might not be safe for discussing the topic of your brother. I wouldn't have let him inside, especially not without your uncle's knowledge and consent, but Audrey had no way of knowing my misgivings."

"You have misgivings?" I asked.

"It's really not safe here," Steph said, but gave my hand a squeeze. A squeeze that was a silent promise that we would talk about it later.

But if the bookshop wasn't safe, that left only the Tower.

201

And I knew we wouldn't both be heading there straight away. "You have to talk to the Wizard first, don't you?" I guessed.

"I'm afraid so," he said. "But once I'm there, I'll send Houdini home to you."

"Well, that's something," I said. It had only been a matter of hours that we'd been apart. But those hours had added up to one very long day.

Once we were above ground inside the hedge maze, Steph said his goodbyes, then teleported into the Tower directly from where we were standing beside the grate. That left me to walk alone back to the bookshop. Once again marveling at how little time had passed while I had been packing every second with action while in dark places.

It was all a little disorienting.

I was just letting myself in the bookshop's Square-facing door when I heard the familiar sound of Houdini's soft paw steps on the grass behind me. I turned to give him a smile, but knew at once that as upset as I was at the loss of the book and the knowledge it may have contained, Houdini was the one more in need of comfort in that moment.

"I guess you heard from Miss Snooty Cat," I said as I bent to scoop him up. He tucked his head under my chin, an angle that didn't let me see his face. But his ears were drooping, and so was his tail. What should be a tightly wound corkscrew was now a limp rope draped over my arm.

"Yes and no," he murmured in the back of my mind.

"Let's go upstairs and get a little food, and then you can tell me all about it," I said as I carried him up all the flights of stairs through the seven levels of the bookshop to my uncles' apartment. Once inside the kitchen, I set Houdini down on the floor, then filled his bowl with kibble. He took a mouthful, but then dropped it to the tile floor to lick at it in a particularly unenthusiastic manner.

"What happened?" I asked.

"She came to see me inside the Tower while the Wizard was

napping," Houdini said, nosing the uneaten kibble away so he could slump to the floor properly. "So *she* never needed an invitation to get inside, apparently."

"You and I are a different sort than she is," I told him. "It might just be a sign that the Wizard doesn't consider her kind anything to fear."

"Maybe," Houdini said. But he sounded at least a little cheered by my words.

"What did she say?" I asked when he didn't go on with his story on his own. "I'm guessing it wasn't good news. But is it bad news, or just 'she couldn't find anything' news?"

"I don't know if it was good or bad," Houdini said. "She had it all with her. An entire packet of parchment, all bound together and sealed in wax. It looked terribly official, but from what office I couldn't even guess."

"And she didn't let you have it?" I asked.

"No, she did not."

"Then why did she even bring it?" I asked, wishing Miss Snooty Cat were there so I could ask her the question directly.

"She said she wasn't sure if she should show me or not," Houdini said miserably. "And then she said that the moment she saw me there, inside the Tower waiting on the Wizard's beck and call, she knew the answer was she should not."

"What?" I asked.

"And she threw the whole packet into the fire. It went up at once, a gust of flame that left nothing but ash," he said.

Well, I knew exactly what that was like.

I picked him up from the floor and carried him into the living room so I could sit on the couch with him on my lap. We sat quietly together for some time. I stroked his back over and over, but the sporadic shivers that rocked his little body never seemed to cease.

That could've just been his rat terrier-chihuahua blood.

But I was pretty sure at least some of it was his sorrowful mood.

"If she found out what you are, then what you are is a thing that can be found out again," I said at last.

But I was also thinking of that book. Whatever that ancient mathematician had deduced about chaos and order, he had worked from older texts. And most of those had surely been destroyed by the censors and the High Council.

But maybe not all.

"That packet looked very old and very official," Houdini said. "I don't think there are two like it. I think she found the one answer, and then she destroyed it. And she wouldn't tell me why."

"It sounds like she didn't like you being so close to the Wizard," I said. "Do you think she has a reason not to trust him?"

"If she does, it's only proof that she truly is an evil creature," Houdini sniffed. "The Wizard wasn't napping the entire time I was there. Most of the time, we sat and talked together. He may be a very great wizard, but he's also a good man."

"I got that sense as well," I said. "From my short time with him, but also from how Steph speaks of him."

We sat together in companionable silence for another long stretch of minutes before Houdini stirred again. "I think what she found must have been something good. Or, at least, something important."

"Why is that?" I asked him.

"Well, I did try to save it, before it had quite burned away," he said. "I jumped into the fireplace and tried to stamp out the flames, but the fire had consumed it too quickly. Not naturally, even for a fire started from a magic spark, you know?"

"I do know," I said, once more thinking of that book. The book and Antonio both. Fire just didn't burn that fast on its own. Not even magic fire.

"I burned my paws a little. It's okay now," he hastened to add as I bent to examine the pads of his feet. "The Wizard put a poultice on them after Miss Snooty Cat left, and they feel just fine now. But when they were still hurting, she laughed at me. And then she said it didn't matter anyway, because she was sure none of it was true. She was sure what she had found was all nonsense."

"She's a cruel beast," I said.

"Yes, but I could tell when she said it that she was lying," Houdini said. "I think, whatever she found, it scared her. Something about me scares her. But what could that possibly be? I mean, if she already knew I was a dragon. What could be scarier than being a dragon?"

"I don't know," I said, scratching all around his ears without touching the ears themselves. "But if she's afraid of you, I think that means not only are you something powerful, like a dragon. You're also something noble."

"Like a dragon," Houdini said.

"Like some kinds of dragons," I conceded. They weren't all one thing or another. Just like people. Or witches. "But we both agree Miss Snooty Cat is trouble. And if she's afraid of you, I think that's definitely a very good thing."

"I agree," Houdini said, but with a sigh.

"We'll figure out who you are. I promise," I said.

"I want to say that it doesn't matter. That whatever I was born to be doesn't mean as much as who I am right now. But I still want to know. You know?"

"Yes, I know," I said with a sigh of my own.

"You didn't get the book," he guessed.

"No, the book is gone. Coincidentally enough, it was burned to ash."

"I'm so sorry to hear that, Tabitha," Houdini said, nosing at my hand.

"It might not have been any use, anyway," I said. "It might have really been nonsense, not like what Miss Snooty Cat found."

"Well, there's another difference too," Houdini said with a growl to his voice in my mind.

"What's that?" I asked.

"She still knows. Whatever she found, she burned the evidence, but the facts are all there in her mind," he said. "There is always a chance I can get her to tell me what she knows."

"Would it be worth what she wanted in exchange?" I asked.

"I don't know," he said. "All I do know is, if she was afraid of who I was before, what must she be feeling now? Now that she's made an enemy of me?"

"All I know is, I suspect our morning breakfast meetings are going to feature a stag Barnardo from now on. So to speak," I said.

"I have no problem with that," Houdini said, and dropped his nose between his paws. The classic sign of him being ready for yet another nap.

I kept petting him even as he slept. And as I watched the afternoon darken into evening, I just kept thinking about a burning packet of parchment. And a burning book of forgotten mathematical theories.

And a glimmer of gold I still didn't understand.

TWENTY-FIVE

I will admit that after the weekend came and went, and I still hadn't heard from either my brother or my boyfriend, I was feeling a little surly.

Well, a lot surly.

I had to keep reminding myself that the week before, I had had neither a boyfriend nor a brother to be annoyed with. So, by some measures, I was still ahead of the game.

But I really wanted to know what was going on with both of them. Because I was starting to get a little paranoid that maybe the same thing was going on with both of them. Big High Council level wizard stuff.

And the last thing I wanted was to resent where I was, in a bookshop, gainfully employed helping people find all the books they never knew how much they'd love.

It was a particularly busy weekend, especially through the prosaic store, and each evening after closing, I went back to my nook to work on tweaking the spell that helped a witch find answers so that it could work for Liam.

Then Monday rolled around with still no word from Steph or Mercutio. Houdini and I went down to breakfast to find Barnardo there without Miss Snooty Cat. Although again, like before, he didn't exactly seem to notice she wasn't there. Only this time, I didn't say anything to him.

Perhaps it was better for him if he thought of her less.

Or else I was being cowardly, afraid that pointing out her absence would end with him going to fetch her. She really was a deeply unpleasant cat. Or matagot. Or whatever.

On the other hand, Barnardo might not have noticed Miss Snooty Cat's absence because he was bubbling over with all the latest blackmail gossip. A few other names had been added to the list of potential blackmail victims/murder suspects, but Barnardo was mostly focused on the still elusive Octavio Manx. Who still hadn't been seen.

When he did mention the Ward family, I shot Audrey and Liam a quick, desperate look. Audrey gave me the slightest of nods, and Liam waited for Barnardo to turn his attention to adding another scone to his plate before doing the same.

I wasn't sure what it meant, suddenly knowing my father's family was one of the most prominent magical families in the United States. But until I knew why it had been kept a secret, even from me, there was no way I would risk letting Barnardo know about it.

I'm sure he wouldn't intend to give me away. But he did like to talk. It was like the truth about Houdini. We were all safer with him not knowing there even was a secret at all.

"But I thought all the blackmail material was destroyed?" Audrey said, and I forced myself to follow the conversation more closely.

"I've heard that rumor too," Barnardo said. "Apparently, the Wizard has been visiting all sorts of nefarious types, assuring them that anything that might have been inside that safe in the repository burned down with the repository."

"What difference does it make?" Liam asked. "I mean, Antonio died, and Prospero was already dead. There isn't anyone left to inherit the family business, even if the blackmail material escaped the fire."

I chewed at my lip, but said nothing. I was pretty sure the Wizard was doing it to protect me, or Steph, or both. In case word got out that we had been in the repository during the fire, then left again before the roof collapsed. He was making sure that none of those dangerous people suspected either Steph or me of having dirt on them.

"What seems silliest to me is what difference it would make to their reputations even if proof did get out," Audrey said. "Doesn't everyone already know these people are bad? Or willing to cross lines in the name of ambition? I mean, Octavio Manx is more the former, and the Ward family more the latter. But everyone already knows this. And it's not like any of it would touch them legally. They're kind of above the law. Unless it was actual murder, maybe."

"Maybe not even then," I said. "Someone killed Prospero, and I really don't think it was Antonio."

But I had no way to prove it.

I fell out of the conversation again, musing moodily to myself until the clock drew close to eight, Audrey's opening time. Barnardo finally noticed he was missing a cat and scurried away to make sure she was all right, all alone in his apartment.

"I should get going as well," Liam said, far more reluctantly.

"Job interview?" I asked hopefully.

But he shook his head. "No, but I can't hang out here all the time. Audrey keeps threatening to pay me for helping out, and I've seen her books. She can't afford an employee yet. Not even one who will work as cheaply as me."

"I can make it work," Audrey said, sounding a touch defensive about her money management skills. "I just don't think this is the job that's meant for you. I don't want you to stop looking for something better suited to you."

"I know," Liam said and nodded, but miserably.

"Look, I finished this," I said, pulling a folded piece of parchment out of one of the many pockets on my capris. I flattened it out before handing it to Audrey. "It's what we were talking about. A rewrite of Agatha's spell. I hope it helps Liam, but no promises."

"We'll have to wait until closing to try it," Audrey said as her eyes scanned my neatest handwriting. "But I already have a feeling for it. There's such a flow to the words, just reading them in my head already feels like magic. You're really something special, Tabitha."

"Yeah, I'm something," I said with somewhat less enthusiasm.

But Liam didn't notice. He just grabbed my hand to pump it up and down in the heartiest of handshakes. "I just know this is going to help me out so much! I can feel it already! Thank you, Tabitha!"

"I mean, even if it works, it's just going to point you in a direction. It's not going to drop a job in your lap," I said.

"I know, I know," he said. "I'm ready for the work, I promise you. I can't wait to do this!"

"Definitely after closing tonight," Audrey said. "We don't want to risk getting interrupted."

"Well, I won't be there, so you'll be somewhat safer on that score," I said.

Liam went to stand by Audrey's shoulder to read the parchment in her hands. Not that the words meant anything to him, but his enthusiasm was palpable. Like it was some sort of force emanating from his body.

I wanted to try warning him again, that magic wasn't something that solved all your problems. Usually, using magic to solve a problem just led to more problems. Half of what we learned in the magical academies was how to use magic, but the other half was when not to. Liam didn't have that training.

But if there was anyone I could trust to reign in any excessive impulses to rely too much on magic, it was Audrey. Liam couldn't be in better hands.

I slipped away unseen as the two of them were still conferring, walking down the prosaic sidewalk to the bookshop. The bell chimed as I came in and turned the sign to *open*.

And found Steph napping behind the apothecary counter.

I almost didn't want to wake him. He was deeply asleep in a way that really shouldn't be possible while perched on a stool and slumped over a counter. It couldn't remotely be comfortable.

But he also looked even more exhausted than he had the last time I'd seen him. Maintaining the magic of the Tower, teleporting without a robe or portal across the entire globe, then whatever he and the Wizard had been up to ever since. It was all taking a toll on him.

Then, in such a Houdini-like manner I nearly laughed out loud, he opened a single eye and looked up at me.

"How long have you been standing there watching me?" he asked as he sat back, rubbing the back of his hand against the corner of his mouth. Not that there'd been any drool.

"I just came in the door," I said. "You could've come to breakfast, you know. You always know where I am at this hour."

"Yeah, not up for a crowd. Not even that one," he said.

"I've heard the Wizard has been meeting with other blackmail victims," I said.

"Not so much meeting as getting the word out," he said. "That's almost exactly the right way to say it. Well, it was a few words, but it was a very brief message sent to all of them remotely. Because taking a meeting would be admitting there was something to meet about. And the Wizard has been too busy for running around, anyway."

"So you've been in the Tower this whole time?" I asked, trying not to feel hurt. That's usually where he was when he wasn't with me, after all.

But he was shaking his head. "No, we were both in Geneva for the last three days. We just got home a few minutes ago. I don't know what you call it when there's no jet involved, but there is defi-nitely a lag."

"You look tired," I said. I couldn't stop myself from brushing some of the hair back from his eyes. Not that my efforts resulted in any kind of neatening of his appearance.

He caught my hand and held it in both of his, pulling me closer, but only so he could speak to me in that smallest of whispers he was so good at using. "Here's the thing. The Wizard is very worried about what happened to you there. That thing you felt in your mind. He wanted to find traces of that magic."

"But you looked and didn't see anything, right?" I said.

"True, but obviously he had to see for himself," he said. Then he laughed humorlessly. "Or, rather, not see for himself. There's no trace of anything. The local authorities are assuming it's related to the taking down of the wards around the Talbot Book Repository. Which we both know it isn't, but the Wizard found it prudent to imply he agreed."

"Well, it's not *not* related," I said. "I was there both times."

"It's possible it was just one or more of the wizards who thought they were being blackmailed, trying to access your mind to see if you knew anything about Antonio or the blackmail materials," Steph said.

"But you don't think so," I said, because that was clear in his tone.

"No," he admitted. "I took your notes, the ones you wrote before Mercutio showed up. You said it felt familiar."

"Yeah, but I couldn't tell you why," I said. "I've thought about it a lot since. I don't think I've ever felt anything like that before. So why should it feel familiar?"

"The spell might have been novel to your experience, but it's possible you felt the magic before," he said, speaking even lower and closer to my ear than before. "Magic feels differently coming from different witches. I'm sure you've noticed before."

"Feeling it is still kind of new to me," I said. "Do you think it was my mother, then? Because it didn't feel like her. Not from what I remember when she tried to put her memory washing spell on me that last time she visited. It was different."

"It might have been your father," he said.

"But I've never met my father," I said. Steph didn't answer. He just kept looking at me with those dark brown eyes of his until I extrapolated the same conclusion he had already come to. "Mercutio said my father took me away. And I don't know what's true because I have no memories before the age of five."

I blew out a frustrated sigh, then slumped against the counter myself.

"Benvolio Ward is a slippery fellow," Steph said. "He has walked a very fine line between being an exceedingly private individual, and being politically motivated. It's... weird. There should be way more information about a member of a council, even one of the smaller ones like Chicago. And yet I've not found out much about him specifically. The family, sure. But him? It's almost like he just barely exists. And your brother even less so."

"My brother," I said, and I didn't even care how grumpy those words sounded. "Nice of him to promise to answer all my questions later, then disappear into thin air the moment 'later' came around."

"Yeah," Steph said, but he sounded distracted. Then he took something out of his pocket and set it on the counter. I picked it up and turned it over in my hands, but I couldn't guess at its function. Most of it was disc-shaped, of a size to fit neatly in the palm of my hand, with a narrow ring around one finger. Only nothing happened when I squeezed it.

Wait, it was gold. Like whatever Steph had taken from the pile of ashes that had been all that was left of Antonio and the book.

"This is...?" I said, and Steph nodded before disappearing the object once before. "What is it?"

He pondered his answer before landing on, "A sort of calling card."

"That?" I said skeptically.

"Antonio had it in his hand. In fact, if the Wizard is correct, he could not put it down even if he wanted to," he said.

"That's what caused the fire? That thing in his hand?" I asked.

"Yes. Antonio might have felt like he was in control, but in the end, he really wasn't."

"So, wait. Someone gave him this thing, and then he couldn't put it down? And then it burned him alive?"

"It burned him to burn the book. Or, at least, that's our theory. But nothing else makes sense," he said.

"That doesn't make sense either. Not to me," I said. "To start with, in what way is this weapon of death a calling card?"

Then I had a sudden flashback. I'd seen something just like this before. The gold joy buzzer that was blocking my view of the titles on the spines of the books in Prospero's office. That had been exactly what I was holding now.

"It's not the first one I've seen," Steph was saying.

But I had to interrupt. "It's not the first one I've seen either. There was one on the bookshelf in Prospero's office."

But to my surprise, Steph only gave me a sad smile and said, "I know. Or, at least, I know now. I didn't notice it at the time. They are used by the Unveiled Guild. They amplify a witch or wizard's own power, to their own demise. Sometimes they retrieve it after, and the death is taken to be a suicide or death by misadventure. It doesn't take chaos magic for some magic users to bite off more than they can chew," he said and gave me a fond smile.

"But sometimes they leave it, and that's when it's a calling card," I said. "Whom do they work for?"

"The highest bidder," he said, and frowned in distaste. "In this case, nearly everyone thought to be involved in the Talbots' blackmail scheme has dealt with the Unveiled Guild at some point. They are thieves as well as assassins. But knowing they are involved simplifies thoughts on what happened to Prospero."

"Someone from the Guild killed him, cleaned out the safe, then burned the building down to cover the evidence," I said.

"Antonio might have interrupted the assassin before he'd finished arranging the scene to his liking," Steph said. "I doubt face-down with a knife in his back was the intended tableau. Or maybe it was, as a warning to other blackmailers. Who knows?"

"Is that our answer to who specifically hired them too? Who knows?" I asked.

"The Wizard was hoping to shake something out when he sent those messages, but none of the responses were particularly revelatory. It was either Octavio Manx or—and I'm sorry to say this—your father."

"Well, I can't get that broken up about it. I still haven't met him." Then another thought struck me. "Mercutio didn't see you take that thing from the pile of ashes, did he?"

"No," Steph said with complete certainty.

"Would he have known what it was if he had?"

"Yes. But would he have admitted to it? That's less clear," he said. He tapped a fingertip to his lips for a moment, lost in thought. It was a rather distracting gesture. But then he leaned closer to speak lowly again. "I've been talking to other ritual magicians about Mercutio. Classmates of his."

"And?"

I almost didn't want to know.

But I *had* to know.

Steph just shrugged. "So far as I can tell, he was well liked. A good student, but not an exceptional one. He did just well enough to get into one of the more prestigious ritual magic graduate programs —although probably with some help from the Ward family—but he didn't exactly excel there, either. If he's currently employed, I can't find out where or doing what. He's an enigma."

"Maybe that runs in the family," I said.

"The Wards are known for keeping secrets," Steph said. But then he looked at me with that dark intensity again. "I think that should include you."

"I'm a secret?" I said. But since no one knew I existed as a member of the Ward family, I guessed that was technically true.

But that wasn't what Steph meant.

"No, I mean..." But he didn't finish. He just swung his foot, kicking the dog bed under the counter ever so slightly. "You know."

"And what about us?" I asked, sliding closer to him. Which almost wasn't possible. "Are we a secret?"

"Us? Not remotely," he said. "I have to keep so many secrets as the Wizard's apprentice, and you have your own, too. Isn't it nice to have something that it doesn't matter who knows about it?"

"Definitely," I said.

CHAPTER

TWENTY-SIX

Even though Miss Snooty Cat would almost certainly not be there, Houdini opted yet again not to come down to breakfast the next morning.

A fact I was immensely grateful for when I stepped out of the bookshop door onto the prosaic sidewalk for the short walk to the teashop to nearly collide with my brother.

"Oh, hello!" he said. For all the world like I was the one it was surprising to find there.

"We don't open for another hour," I said, pulling the door shut behind me and making extra sure I heard it latch.

For all the good it would do if the bookshop felt that this Ward was really part of the Greene-Baxter family, too.

"I wasn't shopping for books. I came to see you, actually," he said. "But you're going out?"

"Just next door for breakfast," I said.

"Right. Audrey and Liam work there," he said, nodding.

"Well, Audrey does," I said. "But Liam will be there too, for breakfast. Is that a problem for you?"

"No, not at all," he said. Then he laughed what was almost a disarming laugh. "I'm actually living out here in the prosaic world, at least for now."

"What?" I said.

I was starting to recognize that if there was anything my brother excelled at, it was saying the last thing I ever expected him to say. All the time.

"Well, I'm sure you know that Mother hasn't been around lately, and our apartment is too big and—well, *lonely*—without her there, too," he said.

"Where has she gone?" I asked.

"No idea!" he said with a laugh. Then, reading the expression on my face, he sobered at once. "She does this. I guess you wouldn't know that. But she does. She flits in and out. When I was a kid, it was deeply upsetting. Just me and the nanny for months and months. But this time, I decided I didn't need to wait around for her to pop back again. I could just... get my own place. Try to build my own life."

"In the prosaic world?" I said, and tried really hard not to sound as skeptical as I felt.

"I'm sure your boyfriend has already told you I'm not working as a ritual magician anywhere," he said. I debated playing dumb, but then found myself nodding. "Yeah. I suppose I could have, if I had been willing to use our family name to open doors. But I tried to do it on my own. I didn't use the Greene name, either. Just a random name, not attached to anyone but me. And, well..." He trailed off, lifting up his hands as if the prosaic world around us finished his sentence for him.

Which, it kind of did.

"Why did you do that?" I asked.

"I wanted to see what would happen," he said. "I guess I found out."

"Just because none of the covens would have you doesn't mean you have to live in the prosaic world," I said.

"Oh, no. That's not what this is about," he said with another little laugh. "I'm not trying to take the Antonio Talbot route. It doesn't work out. Well, he proved that himself, didn't he? He had no protections when he needed them. No support system. Like a naked child out in the cold, cruel world. I tried to help him, but I can't say I'm surprised that it didn't exactly work out."

"I'm sorry we didn't get the book from him in time," I said.

"Oh, that? You know, I never thought it was as important as all that," he said. "I just heard you were looking for it, and then I knew you were here. Bringing Antonio here was just an excuse to talk to you."

"An excuse?"

"To be honest, I thought you'd be a lot... meaner?" he said with an apologetic flinch. "Or maybe moody is the better word. Mercurial? I don't know what I'm trying to say."

But I kind of did. I sighed, then said, "Like our mother."

"Yeah, spot on!" he said with a relieved laugh. "But you're totally not. I actually kind of think you really get me."

"I don't remember anything before the age of five," I said. Or, rather, I just blurted it out. Then I braced myself, waiting for his response.

"Yeah," he said, but this time almost sadly. "Yeah, I don't either. That's messed up, right?"

"Did our mother do that to us?" I asked.

He looked horrified at the thought. And I really wished I could read him, because I was still getting so many little sensations of performance out of him. Maybe he was the kind of guy who was so insecure everything he said sounded like an act. Because he had to put up a front of being more confident than he was.

Or maybe I couldn't trust him at all.

I really couldn't tell.

But I wasn't ready to push him away. I couldn't bear the thought of losing that connection before we'd properly made it.

But I would have to be careful. For my own sake, as much as for Houdini's.

"She wouldn't do that," he finally said. "Our mother isn't perfect, but she isn't evil either. I don't know what happened. I was kind of hoping you did, but I guess we're both in the dark. But maybe we can find our way out of the dark together?"

"Maybe," I said. A look of hurt flashed through his blue eyes, but he just nodded his acceptance. "So you're going to be living in the neighborhood for a while, then?" I asked.

"Yeah. I thought about getting a place inside the Square, but I didn't want you to feel like I was crowding you. I know this place is important to you," he said.

"Thanks," I said. "Although there are so many people living inside the Square, I don't know how one more could feel like crowding. But I appreciate the thought."

"Cool!" he said, relieved again. "I was hoping you'd be okay with it. I really don't want to go back to Chicago. I was all alone there. I know it isn't cool to say so, but I really miss the academy. Not the schoolwork, just the constant presence of other people. Sleeping near others, eating together. All that."

I nodded, although the presence of other people had never been a highlight of my own academy days. No, I'd pretty much relied on the schoolwork to say sane.

But for the first time, something he was saying to me felt a hundred percent sincere.

He was lonely.

And I knew exactly what that felt like.

"As long as you're in the neighborhood, you have a standing invitation to breakfast if you want it," I said, and tugged at his sleeve until he started walking with me along the prosaic sidewalk to the door of the Loose Leaves Teashop.

"You hang out with your friends every day?" he asked.

"Well, the weekends sometimes get busy, but almost every day," I said. "And sometimes, we solve mysteries. But mostly we just chat. Audrey and I work on spells together. The two of us answer all of Liam's questions about the magical world. And Barnardo gives us all the gossip."

"And Steph?" Mercutio asked as we reached the door and I knocked briskly.

"Steph usually can't make it," I said. "But sometimes I bring my dog."

"You have a familiar?" he asked, impressed.

So impressed, I almost hated to admit it. "No, not a familiar. Just a companion. An ordinary rat terrier-chihuahua mix. But I can't get to sleep at night if he's not there, curled up beside me."

"I've always wanted a dog," he said. "Not so much a familiar. That kind of bonding and sharing responsibility is not really for me. Just a dog."

What he didn't say, but I heard anyway, was "for companion-ship." He wanted a dog to take the edge off his loneliness.

"If you like, I'm sure Liam knows where the nearest adoption center is in the prosaic world," I told him. "Unless you wanted a magic dog?"

"No, a prosaic dog sounds just perfect," he said. "I can't wait to meet yours."

Then Audrey opened the door, in midsentence with something she was saying to Liam across the room. She saw Mercutio standing behind me and her eyes widened in surprise. But that quickly morphed into a smile of welcome.

Watching everyone fuss over my brother, fetching him tea and pressuring him to try all the varieties of scone on the serving platter, it felt like I was making the right decision. I could believe he was as lonely as he said. It was the single thing about him that I was abso-lutely sure about. And the only thing better than a dog was a group of human friends.

And there was no reason he couldn't have both.

But a group of friends, a dog, and a sister? Well, I honestly didn't even know what it meant, to be a sister. He probably felt the same way about being a brother. That was going to take slow, careful work, building that relationship.

But also, lingering in the back of my mind, were so many questions about my magic. About his magic. And about how the two of them interacted with each other.

We had so much work before us. So much to learn and talk about and feel our way through.

But for the moment, tea and scones and laughing conversation were enough to get started with. And from the quick, grateful looks he kept shooting me as he chatted with the others, I knew he felt the same.

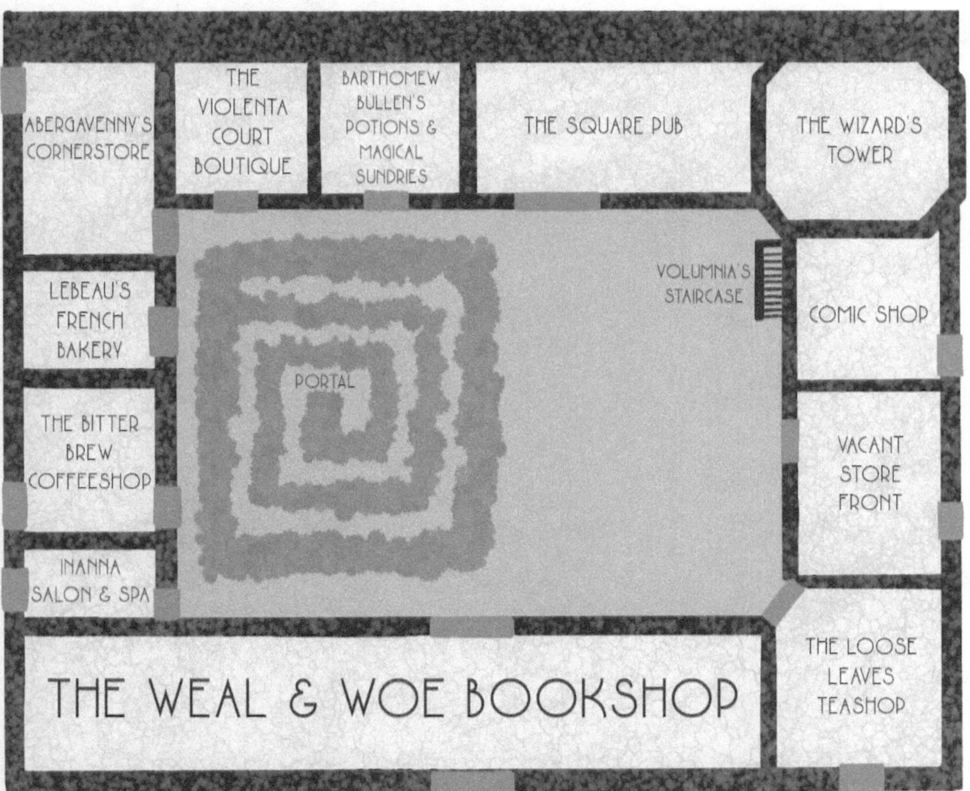

ABERGAVENNY'S CORNERSTORE
THE VIOLENTA COURT BOUTIQUE
BARTHOMEW BULLEN'S POTIONS & MAGICAL SUNDRIES
THE SQUARE PUB
THE WIZARD'S TOWER
LEBEAU'S FRENCH BAKERY
VOLUMNIA'S STAIRCASE
COMIC SHOP
PORTAL
THE BITTER BREW COFFEESHOP
VACANT STORE FRONT
INANNA SALON & SPA
THE LOOSE LEAVES TEASHOP
THE WEAL & WOE BOOKSHOP

CHECK OUT BOOK FOUR!

Tabitha Greene feels blessed by so many things she lacked before. Friends, including a new boyfriend. Family, including a brother she never even knew about. And now she knows her job in the Weal & Woe Bookshop remains hers even when her uncles return from their trip abroad.

She learns more every day about her innate chaos magic, training with her brother and his magic of order. Even Houdini, her little black dog that is secretly a dragon, learns more about his own ancestry when the perfect book finally turns up.

But all of that happiness ends when one of her closest friends is found comatose in his apartment. And beside him lies his equally comatose black Siamese cat, Miss Snooty Cat. Tabitha refuses to rest until she learns just who would harm her friend.

Perhaps someone who knew the secret of Miss Snooty Cat?

THE ENTREPRENEUR ENIGMA, Book 4 in the Weal & Woe Bookshop Witch Mystery series. Available April 9, 2024 direct from Ratatoskr-PressBooks.com or May 14, 2024 in stores everywhere.

THE WITCHES THREE COZY MYSTERIES

In case you missed it, check out Charm School, the first book in the complete Witches Three Cozy Mystery Series!

Amanda Clarke thinks of herself as perfectly ordinary in every way. Just a small-town girl who serves breakfast all day in a little diner nestled next to the highway, nothing but dairy farms for miles around. She fits in there.

But then an old woman she never met dies, and Amanda was named in her will. Now Amanda packs a bag and heads to the big city, to Miss Zenobia Weekes' Charm School for Exceptional Young Ladies. And it's not in just any neighborhood. No, she finds herself on Summit Avenue in St. Paul, a street lined with gorgeous old houses, the former homes of lumber barons, railroad millionaires, even the writer F. Scott Fitzgerald. Why, Amanda can practically hear the jazz music still playing across the decades.

Scratch that. The music really, literally, still plays in the backyard of the charm school. Because the house stretches across time itself. Without a witch to protect this tear in the fabric of the world, anything can spill over. Like music.

Or like murder.

Charm School, the first book in the complete Witches Three Cozy Mystery Series!

THE VIKING WITCH COZY MYSTERIES

In case you missed it, check out Body at the Crossroads, the first book in the Viking Witch Cozy Mystery Series!

When her mother dies after a long illness, Ingrid Torfa must sell the family home to cover the medical bills. Her career as a book illustrator not yet exactly launched, Ingrid faces two options: live in her battered old Volkswagen, or go back to her mother's small town in northern Minnesota.

The small town that still haunts her dreams more than a decade since she last visited it. Or rather, not the town but the grandmother.

All of the drawings she fills notebooks with witches and the trolls that do their bidding? Not as whimsical in her nightmares as she sketches them in the bright light of day.

If not for her beloved cat Mjolner, living in the Volkswagen just might tempt her.

But the cat wants four walls and a door, so north she goes. And finds trouble in the form of a dead body before she even finds her grandmother's little town. How much can a town of stoic fishermen possibly be hiding?

As Ingrid is about to find out, quite a lot.

Body at the Crossroads, the first book in the Viking Witch Cozy Mystery Series!

Also from Ratatoskr Press

The Ritchie and Fitz Sci-Fi Murder Mysteries starts with Murder on the Intergalactic Railway.

For Murdina Ritchie, acceptance at the Oymyakon Foreign Service Academy means one last chance at her dream of becoming a diplomat for the Union of Free Worlds. For Shackleton Fitz IV, it represents his last chance not to fail out of military service entirely.

Strange that fate should throw them together now, among the last group of students admitted after the start of the semester. They had once shared the strongest of friendships. But that all ended a long time ago.

But when an insufferable but politically important woman turns up murdered, the two agree to put their differences aside and work together to solve the case.

Because the murderer might strike again. But more importantly, solving a murder would just have to impress the dour colonel who clearly thinks neither of them belong at his academy.

Murder on the Intergalactic Railway, the first book in the Ritchie and Fitz Sci-Fi Murder Mysteries, available everywhere books are sold.

232

FREE EBOOK!

Like exclusive, free content?

If you'd like to receive "A Collection of Witchy Prequels", a free collection of short story prequels to the Witches Three Cozy Mystery and Viking Witch Cozy Mystery series, as well as other free stories throughout the year, go to my website CateMartin.com to subscribe to my newsletter! This eBook is exclusively for newsletter subscribers and will never be sold in stores. Check it out!

ABOUT THE AUTHOR

Cate Martin has written stories which have appeared in the **Mystery, Crime and Mayhem** quarterly magazine as well as in the annual **Holiday Spectacular** Advent calendar of holiday stories. She is also the author of three witch mystery series: **The Witches Three Cozy Mysteries**, and **The Viking Witch Cozy Mysteries** and **The Weal & Woe Bookshop Witch Mysteries**. She currently lives in Minneapolis, Minnesota. You can learn more about her work at Cate-Martin.com.

Also by Cate Martin

The Witches Three Cozy Mystery Series

Charm School

Work Like a Charm

Third Time is a Charm

Old World Charm

Charm his Pants Off

Charm Offensive

The Witches Three Cozy Mysteries Books 1-3

The Witches Three Cozy Mysteries Books 4-6

The Viking Witch Cozy Mystery Series

Body at the Crossroads

Death Under the Bridge

Murder on the Lake

Killing in the Village Commons

Bloodshed in the Forest

Corpse in the Mead Hall

Slaying on the Lake Shore

Bones by the Forest Road

Sacrifice Behind the Falls

Body Under the Café

Assassination in the Glade

Bewitchment After the Storm

Predator in the Lanes (available January 14, 2025 direct from me or February 11, 2025 in stores everywhere)

The Viking Witch Cozy Mysteries Books 1-3

The Viking Witch Cozy Mysteries Books 4-6

The Weal & Woe Bookshop Witch Mystery Series

The Teashop Terror

The Salon & Spa Scandal

The Bookseller Blunder

The Entrepreneur Enigma

The Novelty Shop Nightmare

The Courtyard Conundrum (available December 10, 2024 direct from me or January 14, 2025 in stores everywhere)